AS BUSY AS A BEE

CYNTHIA TERELST

ISBN: 978-0-648729457

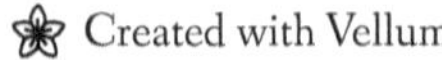

For everyone who believes in love.
For those who share it with me, those who live it and those who read about it.
Without you, my books wouldn't exist.

KEEP IN TOUCH

To be notified of future releases, and to keep up to date with other news, please join my newsletter.

https://www.subscribepage.com/p9p9y0

HART APPLES—Good for your waist, even better for your heart

CHAPTER ONE

Beau

I WAS READY. It had taken me eight years to reach this point. But in each of those years, I'd found strength, resilience and something I'd never had before—self-belief.

I stared out the window. Row after row of bare apple trees stretched before me, the last of the day's light illuminating their starkness. Their uniformity and organisation were calming, though I hardly needed it. Once, my thoughts had been scattered, unreliable. Everything had scared me—life, living, my destiny. But not anymore.

My phone rang and I turned away from the view. It was Mum's monthly call, and she was right on time. The time difference between California and Tasmania was seventeen hours. It was mid-afternoon Friday there and nearly bedtime on Thursday for me.

"Hi, Mum," I said, smiling as her face appeared on my phone screen. I sat on the couch.

"Hi, Beau."

"Have you been busy?"

"Not really, but Dad and I are going to dinner at the Walkers'."

The Walkers?

"It's a birthday dinner for Clare. She's turning twenty-five."

She didn't need to tell me that. I knew exactly how old Clare Walker was. She always celebrated her milestones one year behind me. When I'd turned five, she'd asked, *why do they say you're a big boy now? You're the same size as yesterday.* At ten, she asked, *how's it feel to be ten? If you have two numbers in your age, do you get two scoops of ice cream?* Then, *do you feel all grown-up now you're thirteen? You don't seem very rebellious.* Eighteen, *is freedom calling you?* That was the last time she asked.

"John and Nancy are having a small family dinner for her. You know Clare, she doesn't like big celebrations."

I knew exactly how she felt. But being an only child meant I couldn't avoid them. Moving eight years ago had helped with that, though. My twenty-fifth had been celebrated here, in California, the other side of the world. Mum still made it special by sending some of my favourite foods like Vegemite, Twisties, Cherry Ripes and Milo.

"Beau?"

"Wish her a happy birthday from me."

"She'll be delighted. Remember how close you two were?"

I nodded. I remembered, alright. Images ran through my head—running through the orchard together, doing our homework side by side, holding hands and declaring we could conquer anything together. I shut them down. I needed to stay present for what was coming next. I focused on Mum as I prepared my words. I'd practised them a thousand times. They shouldn't be that hard to say.

"I've been thinking—" Once the words were out, there was no taking them back. "—I've been away for a while. It's time to come home."

Mum's mouth opened and closed. She swallowed. She sucked in a breath. She held her chest. She wasn't having a heart attack, was she? Shit. Where was Dad?

"Mum."

Silence.

"Mum." Louder. I stood up. Her face flushed red, and her eyes were unfocused. What the hell was I going to do from half a world away? Text Dad, maybe?

"Mum. Are you alright?"

She nodded and fanned herself. And then the tears came.

"I'm sorry, Beau." Her voice sounded thick. "We've been waiting eight years to hear those words."

My weak legs lowered me back to the couch. I rolled my eyes and smiled. "Dramatic much?"

She laughed and cried. And then laughed so much she could hardly breathe. She better not bloody choke on the phone. I wasn't going to be responsible for her death. She wiped the tears from her face.

"You're as dramatic as one of those huskies you share videos of," I said.

Her head turned.

"What's going on here?" Dad said, walking into the frame, glancing between her and the phone.

"Beau called me a husky."

Dad's thick eyebrows drew together. "And that made you cry?"

Mum gave me a look that invited me to speak.

I sighed. "I'm coming home."

Dad sunk onto the chair beside Mum. His hand ran through his wavy brown hair. He looked up at the ceiling, and when his eyes returned to the screen, he gave me a nod.

"About bloody time." He put his arm around Mum's shoulders and gave them a squeeze.

My stomach twisted. I'd been away for too long. They missed me. Their sadness was my fault. I pressed my left hand into my leg, hard. No. I'd had to get away. I needed to find my own way. I needed to learn who I was without expectations crushing me—their expectations, my expectations. I was a walnut in a vice. And that vice squeezed, ever so slowly. And ever so slowly, the cracks began to appear.

I always thought I had no control. I thought that everything and everyone was turning the handle on that vice, except me. But I had been with them, twisting it all along. If I hadn't gotten away, I would have cracked into shards.

"When?" Mum asked.

I took a deep breath, and the wretched heaviness disappeared.

"In time for picking season."

Dad nodded, smiling. "It would be good to have another senior on board. You can give Clare and me a hand."

Mum nodded. Her eyes were far away. What was she thinking about? Unease settled in my stomach.

"I don't want a welcome home celebration."

Her eyes focused on me again, and I gave her the sternest look I could muster.

"It's OK, Beau. We know you don't want to be in the spotlight." Dad raised his eyebrows at Mum.

"No. No. I wasn't thinking about that." She glanced between us. "Honest."

What was she thinking about then?

"We need to get ready for dinner. Speak soon." She reached out to disconnect the call.

It was mid-afternoon. They didn't need to get ready for hours. What was she up to?

"No celebration," I said.

She crossed her heart and smiled before their faces disappeared.

I leant back into the soft cushions and closed my eyes. Maybe it would have been better to just turn up on their doorstep. Mum wouldn't have time to prepare anything that way. I shook my head. She wouldn't. She'd respect my wishes.

Was going home a good idea? Years apart didn't mean they'd accept my differences now. They might welcome me with open arms, but would their arms stay open when they realised I was the same person I'd always been? Just because I worked in the apple industry, where they wanted me to be, it didn't mean I'd changed as a person. The essence of me was still the same. And it was always me, the person, that they couldn't reconcile with.

I opened my eyes and went back to the window. The trees here were bare, but back home they'd be green and lush. Apples, the lifeblood of our family, would be growing bigger every day. Dad said he wanted another senior on board. Could I really be considered a senior? I hadn't been there for eight years. I didn't have the experience he and Clare did. What would everyone think? That I walked into the job because of my family connection?

I pressed my hand into my leg. This was the wrong train of thought. I was letting anxiety win. Just because I didn't have experience at Hart Apples, it didn't mean I lacked experience. I'd worked on farms all around the world—Italy,

Victoria, California. I'd worked as a picker, a foreman and a manager. I had experience and I'd prove myself. What they thought didn't matter.

What did matter was how Clare would react.

CHAPTER TWO

Clare

Tahlia sat next to me at the table, her long brown hair shining in the warm light cast from overhead. My short hair would be the same colour as my sister's if I didn't dye it. This week it was red, like the apple in Snow White, like the apples in the orchard. In a week or two, I'd change it to another colour.

She was chatting away about uni. She had one semester left. We didn't mention how she still had one semester left because she'd failed a couple of subjects in her first year. She'd embraced the freedom of uni life a little too much. But that's what growing up is all about—trying, sometimes failing but never giving up.

"Watch out world, Tahlia Walker is coming for you," Pop said from across the table. He gave her a wicked grin.

I laughed. The world sure was going to get a surprise.

Justin and Sharon Hart walked in and headed for the chairs next to Pop. I couldn't ask for better bosses. They helped me develop the skills I needed to be successful. Our families had been friends for generations. Sharon looked different tonight. Maybe it was the energy in her step or her smile that was a touch broader than usual or her bright eyes.

"Hi, everyone. Happy birthday, Clare." She turned her smile on me, and warmth spread through my body. Sharon had the amazing superpower of making me feel it was OK to be me. That I was special. I hadn't always felt this way with her, but time changes people.

"Thank you."

She didn't sit beside Justin. Instead, she went into the kitchen to speak to Nan. Whatever Sharon said to Nan, it turned into a big hug between the two of them. What was that about?

I let the conversation around me dim as I looked around the dining room. It had once been separated from the kitchen by a wall. Nan and Pop had renovated when I'd started primary school. They'd taken down walls, so the kitchen, lounge and dining were one big space. And Pop had made Nan the kitchen of her dreams.

But not everything had been updated. The wooden and glass bureau that held our family china still stood against one wall. When Pop was a kid, they only used the floral dinner set on special occasions. That changed after he came back from the war in Vietnam. After that, Nan said every day was a special occasion. Those were the plates placed in front of us today—white with deep pink flowers and dark green leaves.

My attention returned to the table. Dad and his girlfriend Gloria were talking about house hunting. Gloria said they'd found the perfect place. They just needed to put an offer in. They'd moved in together a year ago. She was alright, I guess. Nothing like Mum, though. My heart squeezed. Another birthday without her, nine birthdays now.

The last birthday I'd spent with her, she was sick. I was sixteen; she didn't make it to see my seventeenth birthday.

I turned my head at the sound of my name. Sharon and Nan were talking and glancing my way. When I caught Nan's eye, she gave me a smile and then whispered to Sharon. Weird.

They brought the food to the table—lasagne, salad and homemade garlic bread.

As Sharon sat, Nan said, "Sharon's got the best news."

Sharon's smile was so big it risked splitting her face in half. "Beau's coming home," she blurted out.

Home? Here? He's coming home?

Nan and Sharon watched me process the news. Why were they watching me like that? I couldn't give two shits about Beau Hart or his whereabouts.

They kept watching me.

I had to say something. "That's great." I hoped my voice sounded more sincere than I felt.

Justin nodded. "He'll be here in a couple of weeks. It will be great having his help."

His idea of great and mine were obviously two different things. I didn't need anything from Beau Hart, especially not his help.

I stared at the plate of lasagne Dad passed to me. I breathed in the rich tomato sauce with a hint of garlic. My mouth watered.

"Aren't you happy Beau is coming home?" Tahlia asked softly. No one could hear over the chatter as they served the food.

"Why would I be?"

Tahlia shrugged, watching me.

I put the plate down and grabbed the bowl of salad being handed around. "If he stays away from my side of the business, I'll be happy." I handed the bowl to her. "I don't need any help. If Justin wants his help, he can have it."

Tahlia laughed. "It's not your business. You don't get to decide where he works or who he helps."

I clutched my fork, wanting to stab someone with it.

I glanced at Nan. She'd gone to a lot of effort for this dinner. And Sharon had this new vibrance, probably because Beau was returning home. Even Justin seemed lighter. Me sitting here thinking selfish thoughts was unfair. I needed to squash my feelings and be happy for them. They deserved that and more from me.

I wouldn't be sitting here now, knowing tomorrow would be another day at my dream job if not for them. I'd just be a high school dropout. I may have made something of myself. I may not have. But their extended hand gave me a future, which meant I needed to suck it up. I needed to put my wants aside. Realistically, Beau hadn't been here for eight years. He had no idea about our operation. And him coming home didn't mean he was suddenly interested in it or that he would stay.

He wouldn't stay.

He wouldn't.

I forked lasagne into my mouth and savoured the richness as it spread across my tongue. Family, love and good food were all I could ask for. My birthday was perfect. That's what this moment was all about. That's what life was all about. Time to get out of my funk.

"Thanks for dinner, Nan. It tastes amazing," I said before I took another mouthful. She beamed at me across the table.

Pop grinned. “She won’t make lasagne for little old me, just you.”

“It’s lucky she cooks it for me every month. Otherwise, you’d never eat it again.”

“Hmph.”

“It’s not my fault I’m her favourite.”

Pop screwed up his face, his wrinkles doubling. Tahlia laughed beside me.

“Don’t tease your Pop,” Nan said.

He poked her in the side and gave her a wink. “It’s OK. You showed me how much you love me last night in bed.”

Tahlia planted her hands over her ears. “Oh my god. La la la.”

Dad shook his head as everyone else laughed.

Family. Love. Good food. That was all a girl needed.

And a job she loved.

That no one was going to take away from me.

CHAPTER THREE

Beau

I LOOKED around the orchard as Dad and I drove in. The rows of trees stretched from the roadway to as far as the eye could see. Red apples, bright and shiny, stood out against the vibrant green leaves. I smiled at the familiarity.

There'd been a few changes in the eight years I was gone. Of course, I'd seen them in photos, but real life was completely different.

"The new machinery shed is over there." Dad pointed to the right. The shed was huge, double the size of the old one, with large sliding doors. "Clare asked for a storage room to be added and an office upstairs for the foremen."

That was a good idea. Foremen in an orchard were usually out in the field but having a place where they could get together to discuss trees, fruit, machinery and workers was important. And a dedicated place to do their computer work was helpful. It made life easier for them and showed them they were valued. One of the problems I'd encountered when I was a foreman was out-of-date and unreliable computer equipment. I'd have to ask our foremen if they were happy with what Hart Apples had.

"What's the old shed used for?"

"We store chemicals and nursery supplies there. Clare preferred that location as it was away from any natural water sources, and runoff would be safe."

Clare. I sat up straight and rubbed my hands on my shorts. I knew she was a big part of the orchard, but I didn't realise how big. It didn't surprise me, though. She'd always been passionate about the orchard. I knew she'd end up here.

We passed a double-storey, blue Colourbond building on the left.

"What's that?" I asked.

"Accommodation for our internationals. Another one of Clare's great ideas. She can tell you about it."

I took a deep breath. I'd be seeing Clare soon. It had been eight years, and she'd always been in my thoughts—our childhood memories, how much I missed her, how important she was to me. In eight years, what I felt for Clare had never faded.

Dad pulled up outside the packing shed and office. It was exactly how I remembered it. A commanding wood and metal building that stood two storeys high with a pitched roof.

Dad turned off the car, and I sat and looked at the shed. Mum wanted me to go into the office first but seeing all those faces for the first time in eight years, answering question after question, was not on my 'to do now' list. My stomach twisted. I was overreacting. Not everyone in there would know who I was or would care. The seasonal staff would have no idea who I was. And once I said hello to the old timers and answered their questions, it would be done with. I could pretend I was meeting all new people, except some would know I hadn't been home for eight years.

Dad pointed at the orchard. "How about you head out to the orchard first?"

He'd become a lot more intuitive over the years. Once, he would have walked into the building, expecting me to follow. I was surprised he hadn't talked about the business the moment I'd arrived home yesterday. He'd always tried to engage me in it before I'd left. But he seemed different. Was it just a temporary change? Where did I fit into it all? I wanted to take my time finding out. Taking my time might be possible if his new attitude was anything to go by.

His phone rang, and he looked at the number. "I have to take this. You go ahead. Water and sunscreen are in there." He pointed to a small side door.

"OK." I hopped out of the car as he answered the call.

I grabbed a box of sunscreen and water from the storeroom and carried it into the orchard. The air was fragrant and sweet. Thick grass between the trees cushioned my steps. This was something I knew and felt comfortable with—helping new pickers settle in and reinforcing requirements. It was the same the world over.

New pickers, which most of them would be, never realised the strength of the Tasmanian sun. Sunburn would haunt them for days. They also didn't think the work was as hard as it actually was. Often, they'd become dehydrated. The days started off cold, and they'd forget to drink. As it warmed up, their layers of clothing would come off, and thirst would start.

My mission was twofold—a mercy mission and a PR mission.

Chatter filled the field. It would die down during the day as the pickers wore out. I walked up the first row, glancing at the apples on the trees. There were plenty. If all went well, we'd have a good harvest this year.

"Good morning," I called out as I approached a group of four pickers, a mixture of men and women.

"Hello," an olive-skinned man said with a heavy European accent.

I looked down at the box in my hands. "I've brought you some water and sunscreen."

"Thank you," he said.

They all approached. Two of them took bottles. The other two indicated they had their own.

I smiled at them. "How's your first day going?"

"Good, good," the first man said, nodding at the others.

"Harder than you thought it would be?"

"Yes," a girl with long, loose hair said.

I didn't doubt it. Their hands would be aching by the end of the day. Their shoulders would be sore tonight from all the reaching and from the weight of the bag they each carried. The straps were wide and padded, but there was a lot of weight in front of you, at least twenty kilograms in each load. That added up over a whole day of picking.

"The first few days are always the hardest."

The lady with long hair kept sneaking looks at me, and when I caught her, she'd give me a smile. My next comment was directed to her. "Make sure to tie your hair back. It will keep it off the fruit, and it won't get tangled in the branches."

"Yes, sorry."

Her apology indicated that the foreman had told her of the requirement. For some reason, she'd chosen not to listen. I'd suggest to the foreman that we watch her closely. If she didn't pay attention to that simple instruction, she mightn't listen to others.

"Do any of you need sunscreen?"

They came forward, and I squirted some into their hands. "Remember to keep drinking water. Have a good day."

I dipped my head at them before making my way to the next pair. I gazed around at the trees; I could be at any apple orchard around the world right now. But in any other apple orchard, the trees surrounding me would not be trees I'd planted as a teen. From small, spindly trees, they'd become strong and productive. At one point, I didn't think I could be either of those two things. I straightened my back. We had come so far.

"Good morning," I said as I approached the two pickers.

One of the workers was emptying his bag into the bin. He placed it down slowly and gently and released the apples. It was excellent technique, ensuring the fruit was not dropped or bruised. People didn't realise how easily apples were bruised. And a bruised apple was no good to anyone.

"My name is Beau. This is my family's orchard." I didn't know how to introduce myself. It wasn't like I had an official title I could announce.

The worker glanced at me and said hi before checking the bin for leaves, wood and blemished apples. He didn't seem like a first-timer. The other picker approached the bin.

"Is this your first year on the farm?" I asked them.

"No, we have been here three times before. We come for six months," he said in broken English. That was interesting. Six months probably started during thinning and ended with picking.

"That's great. Thank you for working on our farm."

He nodded. I needed to find out more about these workers. They could make all the difference. They'd bring their experience back every year and would build on it.

"Do you need any water or sunscreen?"

The second man shook his head. "She'll be apples."

I grinned. It was Dad's favourite saying. As I walked to the next group, I saw someone standing at the end of the row. My heart raced. I recognised Clare straight away by her stance alone—legs spread, feet planted firmly, standing tall and straight, arms crossed.

I waved at her to come over. Bursts of light spread through my chest. Clare was my person, the one I'd always trusted. Until we'd drifted apart. OK, there was no drifting. It was an instant chasm. Could we go back to what we'd been before I left? She was one of the reasons I'd returned. The main reason.

As she got closer, I was confronted with the Clare Stare—jaw set, hard glare, almost a sneer on her face. Her stare was a direct contrast to her stunning golden hair colour, which gave off angelic vibes. I gulped down the lump in my throat. Holy shit, she was angry with me. I should have expected it after what I'd done.

CHAPTER FOUR

Clare

"Hi, Clare," Beau said.

Same wide grin. Same intense green eyes. Same stupid ear piercing I'd given him as a teen. Just older. And not the Beau I once knew.

"Beau." My voice was as hard as I imagined my stare was.

One hand moved to his leg and rested there while the other held a box. "It's great to be back."

"Uh-huh."

"I've missed it here."

If he missed it so much, why did he stay away for eight years?

I swear if he said he'd missed me, I'd punch him in the face.

His grin shrunk to a small smile.

I needed to lighten up. The workers didn't need to see animosity between us. It wasn't professional. I glanced at the box he was holding—water and sunscreen. It was exactly the same as the box I was about to collect. Did he think he could just come back here and take over? Like hell. This wasn't his tradition anymore, not since he decided to leave.

"Do you want to join me?" he asked.

Stuff that. I glanced at the box again. I couldn't leave this up to him. It was my duty to meet the pickers, make them feel welcome and tell them how important they were to this family business. I had plenty of other things to do, away from Beau and his stupid familiarity, but meeting the pickers was important. More important than getting away from Beau. I could collect a box and go out on my own, but I should keep an eye on him. I didn't need him undermining my position.

"Clare?"

My eyes flitted to his face. My stomach did a somersault.

"Shall we go?"

"Sure."

We walked up to the next group, him on one side of the row and me on the other. I needed the distance. I studied the apples on the trees, peered closely at the waste on the ground, looked anywhere but at him. Except for the sneak peeks. I couldn't help those.

"Do you remember how we helped out on summer holidays?" Beau asked from the other side of the row.

I nodded. I didn't want to remember...anything.

"Pop had to make the bags smaller because they were too big and bulky for us," Beau said. "When we got to the bins, the apples would practically drop in."

I clenched my teeth. Memory lane was not where I wanted to be. Maybe I could drop him in a bin. I hid my smile at the thought.

"He told us to put apples in bins that were nearly full, so the apples wouldn't bruise. And then he'd check up on us to make sure we always cleaned our bags."

I didn't trust myself to speak, so I just nodded. It was something we instilled in our pickers to this day because any debris left in the bag could cause damage.

"Hi guys, how's the picking going?" Beau approached the pickers, four women. They gravitated towards him like bees to apple blossoms. A blonde smoothed down wisps of hair that had escaped her ponytail. She couldn't take her eyes off him. The others hung off every word he said. For fuck's sake. He wasn't irresistible. I could resist him just fine.

I went to check their bin while he handed out water. They'd done a great job. The apples were the right size and colour, free from any cracks or bruises. I went back to the group. Beau was still talking, his tone rich and smooth, more cultured than it was when he left. We didn't have all day. Well, maybe *he* did. The rest of us had responsibilities. I bit the inside of my cheek. It was a technique I'd taught myself. It gave me a moment to leave the frustration, come back into myself and stop any rash words.

"Ready?" I asked him.

He nodded without hesitation. "Nice to meet you all."

I headed off, rolling my eyes as they all replied sweetly, "You too." Obviously, I'd need to keep him in check if we were going to get through this section of the orchard any time soon. If I was going to get away from him any time soon.

"I KNOW YOU'RE UP THERE," Pop said from under the tree.

"Yeah, well, it's my thinking place. I'm thinking."

Smoke reached my nostrils, a smell I was familiar with. I imagined Pop down below in his bee suit, smoking the hives. He would have smoked his hands as well to prevent the bees from stinging. He preferred that to wearing gloves. I sat, leaning against the wall of the treehouse and stared at the opposite wall. It was Beau's first day back and already he was disrupting my peaceful routine. I'd managed not to engage in much conversation with him—walking off when he got stuck talking or walking fast between pickers and avoiding eye contact with him. Thank goodness Justin had kept him busy for the rest of the day after we'd finished our rounds.

"Still thinking?" Pop called out.

"Yes."

"About?"

"Things."

Pop didn't say anything. The lid of the hive cracked. Pop would have inserted the hive tool in the small crack between the lid and the hive box to lever it open. Another crack, but quieter this time.

"Beau. I was thinking about Beau. It's his first day back, and he's already inserted himself where he's not wanted."

Pop laughed. "Inserting himself, is he?"

For fuck's sake. Trust me to use a phrase with a double meaning. And trust Pop to point it out.

"He was out this morning with the pickers, giving them water and sunscreen."

"And that's a problem, why?"

It wasn't the actual task that was a problem.

"I didn't need his help."

Pop laughed again. "You don't need anyone's help."

I rolled my eyes. "He was more of a hindrance than a help. All the girls fawned over him, and the guys wanted to chat. Who's got time for that shit? It took way too long to complete a simple task."

It was like when we were kids. Everyone would stop to talk to Beau. I'd always be pulling on his arm, dragging him along, cutting their conversations short. Beau was always thankful that I'd saved him. If he wanted saving this time, I wasn't going to be the one to do it.

"I'm afraid your grandmother was one of those girls."

"What?"

I moved closer to the entrance so I could hear him better. He was looking down at the frames, loosening them, while the tree towered over him. We called this tree Nan and Pop's tree. They planted it together on their wedding day over fifty years ago. It was as strong and healthy as their marriage was. When we were kids, Beau and I took it over. We may have been strong then, but now we were like a rotten tree.

"He came to visit earlier."

What the hell for? It was bad enough I had to deal with him at work; now he was annoying my grandparents?

"Nan thinks he's quite handsome. Do you know what it's like to watch your wife of fifty years gushing over someone young enough to be your grandson?"

He was winding me up. I was sure of it. I wasn't going to respond to the comment. It would just urge him on.

Sure, Beau was handsome if you liked the messy hair, big smile, charming type. I guess his wide shoulders could be considered masculine and appealing. And yeah, those intense green eyes could capture you. But he wasn't perfect. He had a slightly crooked incisor in that toothy smile.

And then there was his ability to abandon people.

He wasn't perfect at all.

"What did he want?"

My legs dangled through the hole. Pop peeked up and gave me a wry smile.

"To say hello."

I gave him a hard stare.

"What? That's all he wanted. He asked about Nan's garden and about my bees. He remembered everything I ever taught you both about bees."

Beau's wide grin the first time he'd pulled a frame out of the hive box flashed through my mind. The freckles across his face matched mine from our sun-kissed days. I shook the memory away. Memories weren't helpful. They'd distort the reality that Beau couldn't be trusted.

"I wish he would remember to leave again."

Pop's eyes snapped up to mine. My stomach tightened. I don't know why I had to feel guilty about my feelings, as ungracious as they were. I understood why he'd had to leave. We'd spoken about it many times. And I knew it was the best thing for him to do, but the way he'd cut me off when he did had torn at my soul. It'd altered my whole being.

I sighed. "Or maybe he can just leave me alone."

"He works here now. You may have to learn that you can't be in charge of everything."

I held his gaze. I didn't want to share anything with Beau Hart. Not memories. Not friendship. Not responsibilities. Nothing.

"You've had control of everything in your life for the past ten years since your mum got sick. It might be nice to share some of the load."

Not with Beau.

He left months after Mum died. He offered to delay the start of uni so he could be there for me. But Mum had been sick for so long that her death wasn't unexpected. I didn't see the point of him staying. But then things had turned to shit. When I needed him the most, he wasn't there for me. He wouldn't even return my call.

I was trying to keep everything in order at home. But order turned to disarray. Tahlia went off the rails. Her actions were driven by her desire to tell the world to go fuck itself. She skipped school. She was angry, sullen and wild. My energy was focused on her and trying to help her find her way in our upside-down world. To keep her at school and focused on her future.

Dad couldn't deal with it, with anything. He was the opposite of Tahlia. He sank so far into himself that I thought he might never come out. All I could do for him was set him on a daily path and make sure he had what he needed.

And in the middle of it all was me. My schooling suffered. I couldn't deal with that and everything else. So, I didn't. I left.

Life was out of control and Beau hadn't been there for me. He didn't share my load then. He wouldn't share my load now.

CHAPTER FIVE

Beau

I WALKED through the packing shed and made my way to the stairs that led up to the office. The noise was constant as apples went from the bath onto a roller belt that moved them out of the water. Brushes removed any remaining leaves and debris. At inspection tables, employees removed apples with sunburn, markings, inconsistent colours and blemishes. Many of the orchards I'd worked on were modern and used technology for sorting. It wasn't left to the human eye. Machines sorted, graded and even had an imaging system to check the apples internally for core rot.

I made a point of not making eye contact with anyone, though I needn't have worried. Everyone was so focused on their tasks that they didn't notice me. There would be no lengthy conversations like yesterday. There was only one person I wanted to have a lengthy conversation with. From her reaction yesterday, though, she wanted anything but.

"Good morning, everyone," I called out as I kept my focus on the stairs. A chorus of hellos followed.

I took hold of the metal banister and made my way up the stairs. A chill ran up my arm. It may have been summer in Tasmania, but the mornings were still fresh. I lifted my hand and placed it down again, relishing the coolness. It kept my mind on the here and now.

Dad's office was on the left. I made my way there and found him bent over paperwork. I knocked on the open door to alert him to my presence. He looked up and smiled.

"Beau, great, you're here." He stood up. "I've set a desk up for you in Clare's office. Follow me."

Clare's office. It didn't surprise me that she'd made her way through the business and was now operations manager. She'd always declared how much she loved the orchard and that she'd work here like her grandfather and father had. I didn't share her love or dreams.

The moment I was able to leave, I did. I could have gone to uni in Hobart, but it was too close to home. I needed to be free. Free of the orchard, free of the expectations. I went to Melbourne instead. Homesickness had hit hard. I'd denied what it was. I'd denied it for a long time. Just like I'd denied my love for the orchard. Just like I'd denied...

"This will be your desk." Dad pointed to the desk on the right. The desks butted up against each other, our computers back-to-back. I glanced at Clare's side. It was practically as bare as mine except for a small pile of paperwork to the left of her keyboard. I smiled. It was like her desk had been at her home, nothing out of place.

Dad walked to my chair. "You've got access to all our data. Start where you like to re-familiarise—"

"What's going on here?" Clare stood in the doorway, her calculating eyes moving between us and the desks.

"I've set Beau up in here. It will be easier for you to share knowledge this way."

Clare crossed her arms. The look on her face went beyond the Clare Stare. If she could have stabbed me right there, using a pruning saw through the eye, she would have. Hell, the daggers she shot at me were enough for me to want to step behind Dad.

"Did you forget to ask Clare if I could move in?" I tried to keep my voice light.

Dad looked between us. It was his business, and he could decide who sat where, but the least he could do was ask her, not just invade her space.

He gave us a wry smile. "I thought it was a good idea."

Clare unfolded her arms. Her face didn't soften.

"Sorry, Clare. I thought it would be good for you to be able to bring Beau up to speed. He's been away a while. Things have changed."

Clare kept her eyes on Dad and gave him a small nod.

"And he can share information with you too. He's been working in the industry in other countries. It would be useful to learn how they do things."

Clare didn't say a word. She just went to her desk and turned her computer on.

"Mum said she'll be here at 12:30 for lunch." Dad walked to the door as I sat down at the desk.

"OK," I said as he left.

"She's wanted to have every meal with me since I got back," I said across the desk.

Clare didn't look away from her screen. "I guess that's what happens when your only child disappears for eight years."

There was that pruning saw again. This time it went straight for the heart. How many times was she going to stab me with it? Was that why she was being so cold with me—because I'd left? I thought she'd understood. It's not like she didn't know I'd been unhappy, that I'd felt trapped. But I'd be stupid to think that was the real reason she was angry. I knew I had a lot to make up for.

I turned my computer on and entered my login details from the sticky note Dad had handed me. I tried to navigate my way to some useful information. It was impossible.

"Where do I find the crop and yield information?"

"I'll email you the link, so you don't need to ask me again."

I stared at my screen. How were we going to work together if she wouldn't even speak to me? I guess it was hard for her to have me in her space, but there wasn't much I could do about it. What Dad said was right. As operations manager, she would be a good source of information. She knew the business inside and out.

So much for taking my time settling back in.

Maybe I shouldn't have stayed away so long but being away had shown me my path. The eight years weren't a waste. I'd earn my place back here. I could add value. And Dad seemed to think so. He'd said I could share things with Clare, as if what I had to say actually meant something.

When I'd first moved away, the thought of going near an apple orchard turned my stomach. I'd wanted to learn about the environment and enrolled in environmental science at uni. But that didn't go to plan. I was lost without Clare. I left in my first year. I gravitated to the only job I knew—apples. At first, I was indiscriminate about where I worked, but as time went on, I chose farms that followed environmentally friendly practices.

The farms I worked on promoted an ecological approach to farming. They encouraged biodiversity and biological control methods. They recognised the importance of bees to their orchards and installed hives. I supplemented my hands-on learning with courses from universities around the world.

Whenever I moved to a new orchard, I made sure they'd be open to these methods. And they were, even the huge orchard I worked on in California. It wasn't at the same level as the smaller farms, but I was still able to make a difference. I could do the same here. Dad's earlier comments gave me hope he would embrace these ideas and changes. That's why after eight years, I'd decided to come home. That, and Clare.

I'd show her I deserved to be here.

I looked through the data, getting lost in the figures. I wrote notes and a list of questions. All the while, Clare was silent. With me, anyway. Her phone rang constantly. I listened to another of her conversations.

"Hey, Dan." Her voice was cheerful.

A long pause.

"I'd just like to remind you that it was your idea to give your kids a summer job." She laughed. "Whose crew are they on?"

Pause. More laughter.

"They did what?"

Clare spun around in her chair. Spin. Spin. Her hair, almost the colour of a Golden Delicious apple, was all I could see above her screen.

"Cardboard cut-outs of you? In the trees?"

She hopped up and went to the window. Maybe she was trying to see for herself. The sun highlighted her hair. I couldn't take my eyes off her. Her short hair accentuated her slender neck. She still had double-pierced ears. We'd done the second piercing together. It was hard pushing the stud through the lobe, but she'd stood resolute, gritting her teeth. It was the same tenacity she went through life with.

"This is a you problem, not a me problem." Still laughing, she hung up.

Clare tapped her phone and held it to her ear. She made her way back to her chair. She spotted me, her eyes widening a fraction. My breath caught in my throat as her eyes met mine. Her smile disappeared. I averted my eyes and stared at my computer screen. Someone answered on the other end of the line, talking fast.

"Ah, how sweet revenge is. I need photos," Clare said. The displeasure she'd shown to me a moment before was gone.

"OK, just make sure it doesn't get out of hand. Don't let anyone put themselves in danger just for a laugh."

She tapped her pen on her desk.

"And don't embarrass him." Her voice was serious but still held a touch of humour.

She giggled.

"A game of Find Danny? Those kids are as bad as him."

She hung up and shook her head before turning her attention to her screen.

I wished she could learn to be friendly like that with me. At the very least, we could have a pleasant working environment. I'd spent enough time being unhappy. I didn't want to be unhappy here now that I'd returned. How was I going to break through the barrier? Time. I needed to give her time. And then, I could start to talk to her and placate her anger. I wanted to get back to where we'd been before I left.

"Clare, Beau, it's so nice seeing you working together," Mum said as she walked into the office.

"How are you today, Sharon?" Clare asked.

Good diversion.

"Excellent. The employees on the floor are starting to find a rhythm. The new ones are learning well."

The first few days of picking were always like this. The pickers were finding their own pace, building slowly. It gave the sorters an opportunity to go slow and learn. Not all of them would make it through the season. We couldn't afford substandard product making it to customers. Pickers, sorters and packers were all required to reach a certain standard in their work. We offered support and training, but sometimes that wasn't enough.

"Are you going to have lunch with us, Clare? I made that apple pie you and Beau love so much."

Clare stood up so quick her chair rolled away. "No, I'm going to Nan and Pop's for lunch."

She didn't even wait for Mum to reply before she shot out the door.

CHAPTER SIX

Clare

I WALKED through the back door into Nan and Pop's kitchen. They were in the dining room starting lunch. Pop hadn't worked in the orchard for years, but he still kept the same time routine.

Nan gave me a smile. "Clare, what are you doing here?"

I sat down at the table. "Just thought I'd have lunch with you."

Nan and Pop looked at each other and had one of those silent mini-conversations you could have after fifty years of marriage. Beau and I'd had those types of conversations once. We'd always known what the other was thinking. Now, I had no idea. I hadn't had any idea since the day he left. I shook my head. What was I thinking about him for?

"Is that why you're really here?" Pop asked.

Nan got up and started to make me a sandwich.

"Yes."

He put his sandwich down and raised his eyebrows at me.

"No. I don't know. Sharon came into the office and asked me to have lunch with them."

"And you didn't want to have lunch with Beau," Nan said from the bench.

"No."

"Why not? You two used to be the best of friends." Nan got ham and cheese out of the fridge.

"That was before."

"Before what?" Pop said.

"Before." Before he left. Before he shut me out.

Nan placed the plate with two ham, cheese and tomato sandwiches in front of me. "I'm sure Beau is much better to look at than the pair of us."

I took a bite out of my sandwich so I didn't have to answer. I'd tried not to be distracted by Beau's presence all day. My eyes were drawn to him, like all those people in the orchard were drawn to him. I gave myself a mental kick every time I caught myself looking at him. He was good-looking, but so what? I'd never paid any attention to it before; why would I now? Before, there had been more to him. More to us. Now we were just strangers sharing an office. It was like we'd never—

"Clare?" Nan prodded.

"What?" I said between bites.

"Want to talk about it?"

Did I? If I started, I might not stop.

"I've worked hard to get where I am. Then Beau returns out of nowhere and it's all at risk."

"I don't think your job is at risk," Pop said.

"Really? Then why did Justin move him into my office? Why do I need to share information with him?"

Nan smiled. "Maybe because you're the best person to help him integrate back into the business."

"Beau Hart has never been interested in the business. He's probably here on a whim. Then he'll just up and leave us all again."

I gritted my teeth to shut my mouth. I'd said *us*. I didn't mean us. I couldn't give two shits about Beau or his whereabouts.

Pop shook his head. I stared down at my plate and grabbed the other half of my sandwich.

"Clare, that's not fair. You know he needed to leave for his sanity. You know he's had a rough time."

I couldn't argue with Pop. I couldn't. When he had PTSD after the war, lots of people treated him like he was crazy. Nan stood by him, the man she'd married.

But it was different with Beau. Wasn't it?

I suppose not. He didn't have PTSD, but he did suffer from something many didn't understand, including his family.

Beau had felt pressure from a young age. He was different from his parents. He saw the world in a different way, and they didn't understand that. I don't think they tried. He overthought things a lot, and they didn't understand that, either. The overthinking would sometimes lead to anxiety that they'd put down to him being scared, a feeling they didn't respect. But if they'd taken the time to understand and talk him through it, his fear would have evaporated.

Like that time some sheet metal had come loose on the workshop roof. Justin told Beau to get up there to fix it. I watched Beau's face. His eyes darted from side to side, a sign he was thinking. Thinking about the safest place to put the ladder, how he was going to carry the tools up there, whether or not the roof was slippery and probably a hundred different other things. He needed a minute to process it all. Before I could open my mouth to quell his anxiety, Justin said, 'Just bloody get up there. There's nothing to be afraid of.' I clenched my jaw and stalked off to get the ladder. Beau followed, not saying a word.

Then when there was an inkling that he didn't want to go into the family business and his interests may lie elsewhere, it hadn't been taken well. It was like he wasn't allowed to be the person he wanted to be. And now he was back in the family business. I had no idea what had changed.

"Why did he have to come back?"

"It's his home."

I took a bite out of my sandwich and chewed until it disintegrated. Beau hadn't cared that it was his home before. What had changed?

Why did I even care? That's what bothered me the most. I didn't want to care, and each minute I spent with him, I was more likely to.

Was I being selfish? I took a bigger bite this time. The answer was yes and no. I should be happy for Beau and his family. I should be happy he was strong enough to return. And brave. He was brave. But I didn't need to be happy about his presence or the way it invaded my life. I'd worked hard to get where I was. I got there by myself; I relied on myself. And that could all be taken away because Beau Hart had decided to come home.

I shrugged. It didn't matter. I could show him the whole Hart Apples world. He wouldn't stay.

"Clare?" Nan said, grabbing my attention. How long had I been lost in my own thoughts? I looked up at her. "Give him a chance. It might be nice to work as a team."

I opened my mouth, but Pop interrupted. "I know it's a hard concept for you; you've been in charge of everything since your mum died." He reached out and rested his hand on my arm. "But it doesn't need to be like that. Having someone in your corner can be liberating."

Beau Hart would never be in my corner. He couldn't be relied upon.

AFTER LUNCH, I went out to the nursery. We'd have to replant a few trees at the end of the season, and I needed to make sure we had enough mature stock on hand. We'd have orders from other growers as well that we'd need to cover.

It was quiet in the nursery area compared to the orchard, where there were pickers and tractors. The orchard still wasn't as noisy as the packing shed, though. I loved the fact that at Hart Apples, we could watch a tree grow from grafting rootstock through to a productive apple tree. Each step in an apple tree's life had important inputs that affected its success at bearing fruit.

It was nearly time to start creating the next generation of apples. Soon leaf buds on new shoots would be sliced off and inserted under the bark of rootstock, ready to join into one. It was one of my favourite jobs in the orchard, creating new life. And, even better, we were starting to move away from only looking at productivity and into reducing chemical use. That's why implementing the use of newer rootstocks early was important. We'd been looking for disease-resistant rootstock varieties. Another thing we were looking to improve was canopies. Consistent canopies increased picking efficiency. I was proud to say we were strategic in what we grew based on scientific research and growing techniques.

"Hi, Clare," Charli, the nursery supervisor, said as she

came out of the office. Charli had gone to school with Beau and me. In the seven years since she'd graduated, she'd married, had two kids and been divorced. Her bucketloads of enthusiasm never allowed her to stay down for long. "I wasn't expecting to see you today."

"I just wanted to check we have everything we need for grafting."

She tilted her head. "Yes, we have what we need. Has something changed since you checked last week?"

Last week, when my head was on straight, and I wasn't avoiding going back to my office.

"Thanks, you know me; I always like to double-check."

She nodded and then smiled, her mouth quirking up at one side. "Oh, you're avoiding Beau."

"No, I'm not."

I went to walk off, but she was there in an instant, blocking my path. "What's he like? Has he changed much? Is he still drool-worthy?"

Damn Charli and her endless curiosity. It wouldn't have been so bad if she could hold her tongue, but she always blurted out whatever she was thinking. When I'd first hired her, she told me how surprised she was that I didn't go with Beau when he left. She said everyone from school thought the same thing. I didn't want to talk about Beau then, and I didn't want to talk about him now.

I stepped around her. "Just ignore me while I look around."

"OK." Charli's voice was unsure, but she didn't follow.

My mind kept drifting back to Beau. He was different from the Beau who'd left eight years ago, and it wasn't just his looks. He had this new confidence about him. I saw it in the way he approached the pickers. He didn't avoid lengthy interactions with them. He spoke clearly, made eye contact and always took the opportunity to teach. When he spoke to the foremen, he took it as a learning opportunity, asking specific questions to gain knowledge. But he did it in such a way that the foremen didn't become guarded. They were happy to share information.

It had only been a couple of days, and he was already making his mark. If I could see this, others could too.

I walked around the nursery, not paying attention to what I was looking at. The plants here were in different stages of becoming an apple tree—rootstock, grafted rootstock, trimmed trees, apple trees in training and the finished product waiting to be dug up in winter. The process of creating an apple tree took years, but the result was a healthy apple tree, ready to produce for an orchard.

The sky above me was blue and cloudless. There was nothing turbulent about it. My heart was not the same.

Avoidance was useless. I headed back to the office. As I left the nursery, Charli called out, "Say hi to Beau for me."

I would do no such thing.

CHAPTER SEVEN

Beau

Clare barely glanced at me when she walked into the office. She was rigid, nothing like the girl I'd left behind. I couldn't help feeling it was all because of me.

"Mum left some apple pie for you in the fridge."

She nodded and sat down. The old Clare would have turned straight around, gone to the kitchen and got herself that piece of pie. Did she not like pie anymore, or was she doing it to spite me?

I didn't think we would immediately be best friends like we had been when I'd left. I'd stuffed that up good and proper when she'd reached out, and I hadn't responded. She'd needed me, but I'd been in no state to help anyone, not even myself. I never wanted to go back to that dark place again. If I did, I might not come out.

So, no, I didn't expect to be best friends, but being friendly would have been nice. Instead, it was like she couldn't stand the sight of me, like being in my presence tortured her. I should apologise. But it would be eight years too late. Even so, it was the right thing to do. Except doing it now would appear too convenient, like I was only saying it because she wasn't speaking to me. She'd never believe that I'd wanted to say sorry for the last eight years. Every time I'd thought about it, as time dragged on, it seemed stupid and pointless.

Taking it slow was the way to go, wasn't it?

I rubbed my legs firmly. I needed to stop overthinking. I could get lost in my thoughts forever, twisting and turning them until nothing seemed feasible.

Every moment I was torn in two. My body, my heart, knew Clare. But my mind said I would never truly know her again.

I needed to make a decision and stick to it. If I didn't, my anxiety would wreak havoc. The fact that I'd already thought about this twice today and debated with myself was a clear sign.

Decision made—best not to start with sorry until she was actually speaking to me.

Clare was concentrating on her computer screen. Now would be a good time to talk about the orchard.

"I took some notes earlier; I was wondering if you've got time to go through them with me," I said.

Clare looked at her watch. "I have a meeting with your dad in thirty minutes."

"We should be done by then."

Clare sighed. She rolled her chair to the left, and I mirrored her move. The screens were no longer dividing us. She sat with her hands folded on the desk, relaxed but not fully open.

"I noticed yields have remained steady except when there's a big frost or hailstorm. Tell me about your tree replacement program."

"We monitor a tree's yield season by season, and when we notice a pattern of decline, we replace the tree."

I nodded. That was pretty normal. "Where do these new trees come from?"

Clare sat up taller in her seat.

"We've got an established nursery on site. The trees are grown in optimal conditions to help when they are transplanted into the orchard. We have several varieties in there, and we supply trees to the public and to other orchards. It's another revenue stream."

I smiled. It was Clare's brainchild. She'd come up with the concept during her traineeship. My questions were deliberate and leading. Should I have felt guilty? Maybe. Did I? Nope.

"Dad said the nursery was your idea."

"I got the idea at TAFE. One of our Tasmanian nurseries was closing, and there was a concern from growers about a gap in the market. We filled that gap.

"Then I approached the Department of Agriculture. Because the youngstock is all grown in a controlled environment, they purchase it for environmental testing."

That was impressive. I'd seen an example of the sort of testing the department did on farms around agricultural colleges. Varieties of trees were tested as well as soil temperature, moisture, nutrients and density. Clare was smart. Very smart.

Dad walked in the door, interrupting my question time. "Clare, sorry you couldn't make lunch. Sharon left you some pie in the fridge."

"Thanks. I can't wait to have it for afternoon tea." She gave him a broad smile. I looked down at my hands. It was me she had the problem with, not the pie.

He grabbed a chair and sat between us. "I thought we'd have our meeting in your office, seeing as you're both here."

Clare's smile disappeared. Was it me she had a problem with or me working at Hart Apples? Maybe she thought we wouldn't be able to work together. Apart from the fact that she couldn't stand the sight of me, I was sure we could work together perfectly fine. We could do everything together perfectly fine, *everything*...

Dad clapped his hands together. Thank goodness. My mind was going somewhere it had no right to go.

"Right, we need a plan to future-proof the business."

"Why? What's wrong with the business?" I asked.

"Nothing is wrong with the business as such."

Why was he being so cagey?

"Justin." Clare's voice was firm, and Dad gave a sigh.

"There's nothing wrong with the business. I'm not going to be in it forever, and you two need to think about where you want it to go."

"Us?" Clare glanced at me and then at Dad.

He shrugged. "Well, yeah, you two are the future."

Clare crossed her arms. I tried not to laugh as she clenched her jaw. It was like the time we were told we couldn't go swimming in the river because her sister might want to do the same, and she wasn't a strong enough swimmer. She said we shouldn't be punished because of Tahlia, and her parents should learn to control her better. Then she walked off, went straight to the river and jumped right in. Was she about to defy Dad the way she'd defied her parents?

"Look, profits have been decreasing. Nothing drastic, but we need to start doing things differently. I'd like you two to come up with some strategies."

Clare was as angry as a cut snake, but to her credit, she

didn't say a cross word to Dad. Her fortitude impressed me. She wasn't able to hold back when she was younger. She always had a compulsiveness about her that I admired. And the Clare Stare backed her up every time.

Dad stood up. He placed a whiteboard marker in front of each of us. "Write your ideas up on the board. Discuss them together. When you have a few viable ones, we'll talk about them."

Clare nodded. When he left the room, I said, "I'm glad I'm not the only one you give the Clare Stare to."

"Beau, we're not children, and I'm not your friend."

She stood up and walked out.

THE SPACE within these four walls had been my favourite place in the orchard as a child. Clare and I would spend hours in this treehouse together. We'd read to each other or play games until she became restless, and we'd head to the orchard. The treehouse felt much bigger then, when my legs didn't stretch so far to the other side.

Dad wanting us to come up with ideas worried me. That was a lot of pressure. I was sure I could fulfil his request. I'd seen a lot on my travels. But whether he'd like the ideas or not was another thing. My ideas were always different from his, and they were probably different from Clare's too.

That statement from Clare was like a slice across the jugular. So final.

I'm not your friend.

Footsteps approached. I stayed still as if moving would reveal my presence. A cough. It was Pop. Clare told me he'd had that cough since he'd returned from the Vietnam War.

I couldn't stay hidden. That would be rude. "Hi, Pop," I said through the floor.

"Beau." He didn't sound surprised that I was there.

"Just came here to think."

"It seems like a common practice."

"Did you come out here to think?" I made my way to the entry and started climbing down.

"I often do."

"I'm sorry. I didn't mean to interrupt you." It seemed like I was interrupting everyone lately.

"That's OK. Thinking doesn't need to be done alone."

Pop sat on the wooden bench beneath the tree. I sat beside him. In the years I'd been gone, his white hair had become thinner. His forearms were still defined, but the skin was looser and more wrinkled.

He stared out into the orchard. "How has life been treating you?"

I stared in the same direction. "It's been good lately."

"Good enough to want to come home."

I nodded. "Yeah."

"How are you finding it?"

"Everything is the same but different."

He nodded. "It was like that when I got back from the war. Everything was the same, but I was different. Something had shifted inside me."

Pop never hid from us what the war had done to him. He didn't detail the trauma, but we knew it was there. We'd heard bits and pieces of stories. He'd worked his family orchard but mainly kept to himself. It was hard integrating back into a society where there was such division about the war. It's not like he'd chosen to go of his own free will. He'd been conscripted.

"I'd seen some horrible things, done some horrible things. The people who weren't there couldn't understand."

I nodded. The war inside me was different to his war. My thoughts were like what dragonflies were to bees. Each thought was prey to another thought that was more agile. They could feed on the other in an all-consuming frenzy. I doubted anyone would understand. I doubted Clare would understand.

"Clare hates me," I blurted out.

Pop gave me a sympathetic smile. "I don't think Clare knows how she feels about you. Angry, sad, scared would be part of it."

None of those were positive feelings.

"I didn't mean to hurt her."

"I know you didn't, son."

I started to shake. Tears were forming. I didn't want to cry. Not because crying was weak. Showing your feelings wasn't weak. I didn't want to cry because it wasn't sympathy I was after. The tears were because of the secret I was about to share. Something I'd never told anyone from my old life.

"That night she called, my anxiety had turned me against myself. It hammered me and hammered me with fear and doubts." I looked down at my hands as my fingers picked at the hem of my shorts. "I couldn't see how things were going to improve. I had no one. I had no future. I wanted to die." I rubbed my thighs, listening to the friction of my palms against the cotton canvas. My hands slowed, then stopped, and the sound disappeared. "That's why I didn't answer her. I didn't want her to be the last person I spoke to. I didn't want to carry that guilt into my last breath."

Pop didn't say a word. He just nodded. We continued to stare out into the orchard.

"When I got back from the war, I couldn't sleep. Lying down was foreign to me. I slept propped up in the corner facing the bedroom door. You couldn't call it sleeping. I was always half-conscious. Ready for action. Ready for the enemy."

His current relaxed state was the opposite of what he described.

"Nancy tried to understand, tried to let me know I wasn't alone. I'd scream at her, all my terror and fear in those words. People in the orchard would hear. I'd shut down for days. People in the orchard could see. They would talk. They would shake their heads. They would look the other way when they saw me.

"You know what Nancy did? She told them to shut up and mind their own business. She stood by me. She trusted me."

He turned to me, and our eyes met.

"Clare can be that person for you."

"She always was."

"Clare needs to trust you again. Give her something to trust in. You'll only get one chance at this, or you'll lose her forever."

No pressure.

CHAPTER EIGHT

Clare

I LAY IN BED, staring up at the ceiling. I'd been staring into the darkness on and off for hours. My cat, Clementine, had become fed up with my restlessness and had moved away from me to get a peaceful sleep. With the room starting to lighten, I could see her black body curled up next to the other pillow. I stretched out my hand to touch her, and she made her half-purr, half-chirp sound.

I had so many ideas running through my mind. I couldn't wait to share them with Justin. He said Beau and I had to share ideas, but Justin and I had a better working relationship. It would be easier to talk to him about them. He would understand my vision better.

I got up and showered, and went to make breakfast. Clementine followed me the whole time. She meowed at each step to remind me she needed her breakfast. Like I'd ever forgotten. We ate in silence until I broke it. "Life as a cat is pretty easy, isn't it, Clementine?"

She looked over at me before resuming eating her meat.

"You don't have to worry about work. Or about annoying people. Or about a man who kissed you and then disappeared."

Her ears twitched, but that was the extent of the attention she was willing to pay me.

I tried to wipe away the memory. The memory that had kept me awake last night alongside my ideas. The kiss I could never fully forget.

BEAU STEPPED *out of his car, and we stood under the apple tree staring at each other. I'd always known this moment was coming, the moment he'd drive away and leave us all behind while he made it on his own.*

"Well, this is it," I said.

"Yep."

"I hope you find what you're looking for out there."

He stepped forward and took hold of my hands. A bolt of energy shot through me. What on Earth? I willed it away. It was just the emotion of the moment, the fact that my best friend was leaving.

Beau took a step closer. I looked into his eyes. They searched my face, pausing ever so slightly at my eyes, my mouth, my freckles, before moving on.

He stepped closer again. His features were all I could see —warm green eyes, scruffy hair, full lips. His hands left mine. One went to my waist, and the other cupped the back of my head. My hands fell by my side, empty.

Beau's lips met mine. They were soft, hesitant at first. He moved in closer, our bodies touching. Warmth spread through me everywhere, like my whole body was blushing. I wrapped my arms around him. I didn't even command them. It was like it was their natural place.

His lips, my lips—they opened to each other. Everything I knew about Beau disappeared at that moment, and something primal took over. Kissing him was all I needed. Raw energy spread from our lips through my body. Lightness filled every space, followed by an aching need that could only be filled by him.

His lips slowed and then stopped. My head spun. What had just happened? Kissing was not something Beau and I did.

Beau rested his forehead on mine. Then he pulled away. I opened my eyes slowly as the gap between us increased. I stared at Beau as he stared at me. His eyes were wide, his wet lips slightly parted, and his breathing harsh.

"I love you, Clare."

Before I could say a word, he hopped into his car and drove off.

THE MEMORY NEEDED to stop pushing itself into the forefront of my mind. I shoved my chair back and took my dishes to the sink. There was no point to any of these thoughts. Just like there was no point to that stupid kiss. It was like Beau had been trying to see what it felt like before he left. A test of some kind. It didn't mean anything because if it had, he would have spoken to me about it instead of pretending it had never happened.

I needed to concentrate on the task Justin had given us, not on Beau. I wrestled with my mind all the way to work. Those words I'd said to him yesterday were harsh. *We are not children, and I'm not your friend.* I couldn't help it. Words were my shield, all I had to protect myself. Being dragged deeper into feeling something for Beau other than anger and distaste would do me no good.

When I'd started work at the orchard, I'd kept my distance from Justin and Sharon. I resented them for how they'd treated Beau growing up. It was their fault that he'd left, and I couldn't get past that.

But over the years, my resentment dwindled. I couldn't hold the anger in my heart forever and let it keep eating at me. Beau was gone. They were here. I felt guilty at first like I was betraying Beau, but that guilt didn't last. The longer Beau stayed away, it was less about what they'd done and more about his choice. Justin and Sharon listened to my ideas and respected my opinion. They gave me more responsibility and started including me in decision-making. I was promoted and then promoted again. In the end, my bitterness disappeared altogether.

The office was quiet when I walked in. My office was still dark, but Justin's lights were on. It didn't surprise me he was in early. His door was open, so I walked in and sat opposite him.

"Good morning." My voice sounded too bright, even to me.

"Morning."

"I've got some ideas about the business."

He smiled. "Excellent. Have you written them on the board?"

Damn.

"No, I thought I'd run them past you." There was no point talking to Beau about it. I stared openly at Justin, placing subtle pressure on him. If psychic powers were a thing, I'd convince him to listen to me.

"That's for you and Beau to do together."

I groaned on the inside.

"You and Beau need to work together to help decide the future of the business."

My stomach dropped. I nodded, gave him a smile and left.

I couldn't believe he was serious. What I wanted to do was tell him that he was delusional. Beau wouldn't be here long term. He wouldn't see any of these plans through. But those words would be cruel. He and Sharon may have similar doubts, and to tell them I thought the same would only increase their doubts. I hoped for them Beau would stay.

Those words, though, *you two need to think about where you want the business to go*, made my stomach turn. Like we'd be running the business together. Until he decided to leave, we'd need to work together. And not just together like you would with a co-worker, but closely together as partners. What a nightmare. Would I rather him take over? Fuck no.

I walked into my office and stared at the board. What would Beau think of my ideas? Would he think they were any good? I picked up my whiteboard marker. The whiteness of the board engulfed my vision. There was nothing but stark white. Blank white. Emptiness.

Maybe I should let him write the first words.

Bullshit. My ideas were good. I wrote.

Expand

Automate

Diversify

I sat at my desk and started work, checking the figures from the previous day. They looked good.

"Good morning," Beau said as he entered the office.

"Morning." I gave him a slow stare. He turned to put his backpack in the corner. It was crisp outside, but he was wearing shorts. He'd acclimatised quickly. With his back to me, I could see he wasn't one of those men who had no arse, whose shorts hung off their hips. He filled his out nicely. My eyes drifted down to his muscled calves and up again. He turned to the desk. I averted my eyes so fast I nearly gave them whiplash.

"You've written some things on the board already." He focused on the words I'd written.

"I figured we might as well get started."

"I have some ideas too. But let's talk about yours first."

Why would he want to do that? Maybe he didn't have any ideas, or maybe he wanted to see if mine were better. It would give him time to change his up. I should have held my ideas close, but there was no point because Justin wouldn't listen to them without Beau hearing them first.

"What do you mean by 'expand'?" He must have gotten tired of waiting for me.

"Well, if we bought more farms in different areas, we could increase yield and spread risk."

Beau turned to me. "Spread risk in what way?"

"Climate change is going to see an increase in the frequency and severity of hailstorms. If we have orchards in different areas, one orchard could be hit while another one stays safe."

Beau nodded. "That goes for frost, disease and pests too." He sat down and rolled his chair to my side of the desk. "There would be a cost increase. We'd need to spread our resources further, and there would also be fuel costs between the farms and to bring apples here to be processed."

Those were good points.

"Do you know anything about our available capital or equity? Can we afford to expand?" I asked.

Beau shook his head. He stood up and wrote *more farms*

—increase yield, spread risk next to expand. Then he wrote *capital?*

He turned back to me. "What about automate?"

"Technology is changing all the time. Perhaps we can look at how we can automate some of the activities in the orchard."

Beau paced in front of the board. He was taking this more seriously than I thought he would. "Harvest platforms are good for picking, pruning and thinning. I've seen them used."

"Where?" Idiot. Why did I ask that? I didn't care where. I didn't want him to think I cared about anything he did.

Beau stopped pacing and considered me. "In Italy and California. California was a newer orchard. They'd invested big in technology to lower ongoing costs and increase profitability."

"How did the platforms help lower costs?"

I was interested in the cost factor, not the Beau factor.

"Less bruising, almost down to zero per cent. And they did the same harvest with fewer workers."

That was impressive. Bruising could be a big problem, especially with new pickers who were still learning or didn't care. That's where our international workers made a huge difference. They respected their work, they respected us and they made all the difference. They knew if they didn't perform, they wouldn't return the following year or could be sent home before their time. If Beau was right, bringing in platforms would reduce the number of workers we needed.

"The cost savings would need to be weighed up against the human expense," I said.

"What do you mean?" Beau asked.

"We employ a lot of locals who rely on us for their income as well as international workers. The money they earn here helps build a better future for their families—good schools, opening businesses, building new homes."

Beau sat down. "How much of our workforce are international workers?"

"We currently employ twenty. They've reduced our need for relying on backpackers with no obligation to stay and who, if they find the work too hard, won't."

Beau nodded. "It's the same in other countries." He swung his chair around to the board. "Diversify?"

"Our product. We could also grow cherries."

"On this orchard or a new orchard?"

"Probably a new one."

"I think it's a viable idea. There's been a decline in the consumption of apples in the domestic market. And it's too hard to export to places like China when our production costs are so much higher than theirs. Cherries, on the other hand, have a growing market, and exporting is favourable."

"My thoughts exactly."

He gave me a wide smile, a smile I'd recognise anywhere. My lips curled up. The smile may have been on the face of a man who'd travelled the world, a man who'd won his fight with his internal demons, but the smile was that of a boy who had once been my world. Until he wasn't.

The air was sucked out of my lungs like I was in a Cryovac machine.

CHAPTER NINE

Beau

My whole world brightened with just the curve of Clare's lips. It was the first time she'd smiled since I'd come back.

Clare stood up. "I have to go to a meeting."

I watched her walk to the door. Before she left, she said, "You should write your ideas up."

I wasn't ready to write mine up yet. I wanted to grab onto hers and explore them a little deeper. If I did, maybe she'd smile again.

When we were kids, her smile was all I needed. On my down days it would lift me, get me out of my own head for a moment. Her smile was enough to convince me to do something, even if my head was telling me not to. Like the time we rowed a handmade raft up the river to town because she wanted a bag of lollies.

She'd had answers to all my questions. What if it's not seaworthy? We're not going out to sea; we're travelling up a river. What if it capsizes? We've crossed the river; it's never capsized before. But what if it does? We'll swim to the bank. What if I can't? You swim further than that in swimming lessons. What if I get a cramp? Mum says it's dangerous to get a cramp while swimming. I'll save you. Your dad said not to swim in the river. We're not swimming; we're rafting. When I relented, she gave me a smile.

That smile was all I needed back then. And apparently, that's all I needed now. She'd believed in me once; I needed her to believe in me again. I needed to prove to her that I wanted to be here, with her.

I did deserve to be here, didn't I? I pressed my hand against my leg. I didn't need to keep going over the same thing. I'd answered all my doubts before. Just like Clare had answered all my doubts that day at the river.

I looked at the board. Clare's ideas were solid. How much were they going to cost? I moved my chair to the computer and started researching prices. Every time I clicked on a new property for sale, the price got higher. If that's the way we were going to go, we wouldn't want to wait more than a year to buy.

The equipment, on the other hand, would be more affordable to purchase. I emailed my old manager in California to get some extra information on equipment. Within minutes he emailed back with what I needed and reminded me that there was always a job there for me. I smiled, remembering how he didn't want me to leave. Armed with his information, I made some calls to get more accurate pricing. I wrote prices for new orchards and equipment on the board. Cherries were a good crop option. The harvest wouldn't clash with our apple harvest. Export markets were already good with high potential for growth.

I stood up to write some data on the board.

"I see you've got some ideas on the board," Dad said. I turned to see him standing in the doorway.

"They're Clare's ideas. I'm just getting some costs."

He studied the board. "Of course they are. They're good ideas."

Another point for Clare.

Was he saying my ideas wouldn't be good?

Dad turned his attention to me.

"How are things going with Clare?"

"OK."

He smiled and walked out.

OK was an overstatement, but I didn't want to tell him the truth. In my wildest dreams, I'd imagined coming back and everything being like it always had been. Unrealistic, but dreams often were. I'd played out many scenarios in my head over the years. What I'd say to her, what I'd do when I saw her again. None of them were close to the reality I'd encountered.

Clare was angry, and she had every right to be. I could justify to myself that she knew I was going to leave. But leaving physically wasn't the only thing I'd done. I'd left her completely. No calls. No messages. As my anxiety increased, the possibility of contact disappeared altogether. My head wouldn't let it happen. It told me she wouldn't want to speak to me, that I was a waste of space and she would be better off without me. I didn't return her call when she reached out to me. I couldn't face her or my feelings for her. There was no point. She had so much potential, and I had none. Dropping out of uni proved that. It was another thing I'd failed at.

I hadn't wanted to drag her down with me. She would have supported me, but I couldn't keep relying on her. I was a grown man. I couldn't keep asking my friend for help. She always told me I was enough, just me, but it wasn't true. I'd never be enough. Not for her, not for my parents, not back then. Those thoughts led me down the dark path where I thought death was my only option.

Dad's question ran through my mind again. *How are things going with Clare?* I was fooling myself if I thought things were good. They were far from it. I might hang onto that smile like it was a lifeline, but she could cut the rope at any time. I could have been a lifeline for her when she needed me the most, but I hadn't been.

I had a lot of work to do to make it up to her.

WE SAT around the dinner table, Mum and Dad opposite each other and me on the end. Everything about being home was familiar. Some furniture had been updated, but it was still in the same place. Family photos that had once adorned the walls in an eclectic mix of frames now hung on the wall in uniformly rectangular black frames. It was weird to walk past smiling photos of us. The last photo was from the day I graduated high school. Eight years of me were missing.

My room was practically the same as I'd left it. Except my drawings were no longer on the walls. I'd taken them down and given them to Clare before I'd departed. I'd stopped giving new ones to Mum to put on the fridge after I found out she threw the old ones away. Even my clothes were still there. They wouldn't fit anymore. I'd filled out, and they'd be too tight across the chest and shoulders. I needed to ask Mum for bags so we could give them to charity, but I felt like maybe it was too soon. Maybe she wasn't ready to let go of it all.

I was. Everything was a reminder of my old life. It wasn't all bad, and I had a lot of good memories, but I was ready to leave it all behind. I wanted to start fresh. I'd accepted who I was a long time ago. My mental illness was a part of me. I needed them to accept it, too, like Pop did. Accepting *it* would mean accepting me as a whole.

"Are you enjoying working with Clare?" Mum asked.

"Yes." I didn't elaborate. There wasn't much to say.

"They started discussing their ideas today," Dad said.

"Oh good."

I wasn't sure if he was dropping a hint that they were Clare's ideas and not mine. OK, that was anxiety talking. There was nothing to indicate that's what he meant at all. I needed to keep my anxiety in check. It had been sneaking in ever so slowly. I couldn't afford for it to take hold.

"Clare told me a little about the international workers today. How long have you been employing them?"

"This is the fourth year," Dad said. "Clare organises it all every year. She—"

"You should ask Clare about it," Mum interjected. "She knows the program inside out."

Dad gave her a sideways look. "I was going to say she goes over every year to interview and choose the employees for the coming season. We have a fifty per cent return rate."

I didn't know if that was good or bad, but I was guessing if Dad mentioned it, it was good. I forked mashed potato into my mouth. Could Clare do anything wrong in his eyes?

"When I worked in Italy, the language barrier was a problem at first. I was lucky the younger generation spoke English and helped me learn Italian."

"Our workers have an English class once a week, even before they arrive," Mum said.

"That's a good idea. I struggled at first, but it was important to learn."

Dad grunted. "Glad you had your priorities straight."

That was a good little dig. I knew exactly where he thought my priorities should be.

The non-work talk had only lasted a day. I wasn't surprised. If I allowed it to, the conversation would continue the same way—Clare and work. I needed to change its direction. The photos on the walls watched us, smiling. At what, who knows? Maybe they knew what I was about to say.

"I'll be leaving early in the morning. I want to check out the twenty-four-hour gym in town."

"Oh, yes, that's quite new," Mum said.

"Physical activity is good for mental health. You know, endorphins, serotonin and all that," I said.

Dad nodded while he chewed his food. Mum was silent. I imagined her counting every time her teeth crushed the food in her mouth. *You need to chew your food, Beau. Thirty-two times for each mouthful.*

There were plenty of things they could have asked. What type of physical activity do you enjoy, Beau? What else helps with your anxiety? That last word would need to be whispered as if it were taboo. Are you feeling better now?

You'd think me being twenty-six, it would have been something we'd discussed years ago. But no, it wasn't really spoken of unless Dad was dismissing it. I thought approaching the subject side on would have helped. Perhaps it had taken them by surprise. Maybe they'd thought I'd grown out of it.

CHAPTER TEN

Clare

I WALKED in and sat at my desk. Beau had added things to the board. Not his own ideas but expansions on mine. I didn't acknowledge his work, and he didn't mention it.

This was the old Beau I knew, always supporting me. I'd come up with some scheme, and he'd be there with me, backing me one hundred per cent. Like when the new phase at school was for the kids to play kiss chasey. I was not remotely interested in kissing some boy, even if it was just a peck before running away again. I told Beau I didn't want boy germs and that the only boy I'd kiss was him. His germs were the same as my germs. We did everything together anyway. We might as well kiss, so we didn't have to kiss someone else. He didn't hesitate. He didn't like the other girls with their silly crushes and their stupid comments about him being their beau. He didn't see me as one of them. Our last kiss flashed into my mind. I pushed it away hard and fast as if it were a branch coming towards me while pruning.

I trusted him when we were kids, but could I trust him now? I still didn't know if he was here for the right reasons or if he would stay. He didn't before. First, Mum had left and then it was him. Mum didn't choose to go; she couldn't fight the cancer anymore. But Beau chose to go. And then he chose not to come back.

But he was back now, and if he was back to stay, he should have ideas to share.

"Where are your ideas?" I said across the desk.

"I wanted to get some more data on yours first. We need to look at every aspect."

I guess that was fair.

"What was your meeting about yesterday?" he asked.

"Just a rundown on how the harvest was going."

I hadn't come back to the office after the meeting. I thought my time was better spent elsewhere. That was my excuse, and I was sticking to it.

"And how is it going?"

"Good. We've lost a few backpackers, but we expected that."

"OK."

My vagueness worked in my favour. He stopped asking questions.

I should have invited him to the meeting, but I needed time apart from him. I needed to separate my feelings for the old Beau from the new Beau. And being with him made it hard to do.

I was such a bitch, excluding him because I couldn't deal with my own feelings.

Guilt got the better of me. "What did you work on while I was gone?"

"I did some research on your ideas. Then I looked into what Dad said about profits decreasing."

"What did you find?"

"They have been dropping. I think that's normal if efficiencies aren't put into place consistently."

What was he trying to say? That I'd failed? I clenched my teeth. He couldn't talk. He'd failed in more ways than one.

I took a deep breath. My inner bitch was coming out again. I needed to keep it under control.

"I think the nursery profits boosted overall performance, so it wasn't obvious. And the industry has been working in a tighter market, so a drop wasn't surprising," he added.

So, he wasn't blaming me?

"It's nothing to be concerned about. I think we can turn it around."

We? I bit the side of my tongue to stop myself from saying what I thought about *we*.

POP WAS SITTING under the tree staring out into the orchard when I pulled up into the driveway. He waved to me and stood up. He moved slower these days but was still spritely for a man of his age who'd gone to war and worked as a manual labourer after returning.

"To what do we owe this pleasure?" he asked when he reached me.

"No special reason."

We walked to the house together.

"Nothing to do with Beau, then?"

I shrugged. Of course, it had to do with Beau. I wasn't going to admit that now that I'd been called out on it. "I visited all the time before Beau arrived."

"Uh-huh."

I opened the door for Pop and followed him in.

"Put the kettle on, love. Clare's here to tell us about her day."

"That's not what I'm here for."

"Sorry, correction, she's here to tell us about Beau."

I rolled my eyes and made my way to the dining table. Pop followed.

"How is Beau?" Nan asked from the bench as she sat three mugs down.

"Fine."

"If you're here to talk about him, you need to use more words than that," Pop said, a cheeky grin on his face.

"Beau is fine. I wrote my ideas on the board yesterday."

"And what did Beau say about them?" Nan asked.

"He was positive. He asked lots of questions. He even did some research while I was at a meeting." And hiding from him.

Nan placed a fourth mug on the bench. "Speak of the devil, and the devil will appear."

What? Beau was here? Was nothing sacred?

He walked past the window and knocked on the kitchen door.

"Come in, Beau," Nan said.

He walked in and gave Nan a kiss on the cheek. She smiled in response. Her whole face was glowing, and I was surprised she didn't grab him and hug him tightly like she did when Tahlia hadn't visited for a while.

"Hi, Pop," Beau said.

Beau sat beside me and gave me a sheepish smile. My chest squeezed. What the hell? I stopped myself from moving my chair closer to his. When we were younger, we sat so close together our arms or legs would touch. Our presence, our touch, would mean something different to each of us. His restricted my impulsiveness. Mine kept him level. Both offered a sense of calm.

"Clare was going to tell us about her ideas," Nan said as she brought the cups to the table—tea for her and Pop and Milo for Beau and me.

"They were great," Beau said. "We have a lot to think about."

There it was again, the positivity and support. But no mention of his ideas. I studied him closely. He rubbed his left hand on his shorts. When he turned to me, he gave me a small smile. I was such an idiot. He wasn't keeping his ideas from me out of malice. He was anxious about sharing them. His mind would be comparing mine to his, and he'd be thinking how his didn't measure up. I grabbed hold of my mug so my hand didn't reach out to him.

"Change can be hard," Nan said.

Pop nodded. "When England joined the common market in 1973, the arse fell out of the export industry. That's where most of our money came from. Back then, the apple industry exported six million boxes a year."

Pop took a sip of his tea.

"Six million boxes? We only export a quarter of that now," Beau said.

Pop sighed. "It was a hard time for the industry. Many of our orchards had been in the family for generations. All of a sudden, there were over a thousand commercial apple growers in financial distress." Pop ran his hand over his face. "Yeah, it was a hard time."

"The problem was, none of us saw it coming," Nan said. "We'd endured huge hailstorms the year before. It was hard to come back from that, and then our potential income was wiped away."

"On top of that, I'd just come back from the war, and things weren't going too well for me."

Now I really wanted to reach out to Beau. I'd known about all of this in parts but not how it all lined up in the timeline. I swallowed the lump in my throat.

"Everything my family worked for was about to disappear."

"Pop's parents had already moved to Hobart; they weren't involved in the orchard anymore. It was only Pop and me."

I gripped my mug, holding back tears. Pop had come back from the war, his mind shattered, and then his whole future was about to be destroyed. Beau's knee rested against mine. My hands loosened on the mug.

"The government implemented the Tree Pull Scheme," Pop said. "Basically, the government paid farmers to rip out their orchards."

"Orchard after orchard was bulldozed," Nan said. "Hundreds of them."

Trees would have become nothing but roots and stumps, their vibrant lives turned into nothing but decaying wood. And the lives of their owners, what happened to them?

Nan looked over at Pop and took his hand. "We didn't know what to do. The orchard was Pop's sanctuary. Leaving and living in town wasn't really an option."

He had been suffering a broken life in more ways than one. I could still feel the pressure of Beau's knee against mine. Pop smiled at Beau. "That's when your Pop saved the day. He didn't want to leave the industry. He wanted to expand. He offered to buy the farm from us with an understanding that we'd still live in the house as if it were our own."

Nan smiled. "It was the salvation we needed. We stayed. Pop continued to work with the apples."

"Some days, I couldn't do it. I couldn't leave the house. Your Pop never judged me for that. We didn't know what PTSD was back then, but we knew what it could do to a family. When your great-grandfather came back from World War II, he suffered from it. They called it shellshock back then. He drank himself to death."

Beau and I stayed silent, lost in our thoughts. Once, our thoughts would have been almost identical. I didn't know Beau well enough anymore. We were so lucky to have Beau's family. They supported Pop, they supported Dad when Mum died, and when I needed help, they were there for me too. Was he thinking the same thing?

"Well, that was a bit of heavy talk for an afternoon cuppa," Nan said.

Pop laughed. "Yeah, all I really wanted to say was that change can be good. Not having to run the whole operation while I was trying to get my life straight was helpful."

"It gave Pop time to heal," Nan said.

I finished my Milo.

"Is there anything else you'd like to talk about while you're here?" Nan asked, glancing between us.

I shook my head as Beau did the same.

"Maybe like each other," Pop added.

I clutched my mug and stood up. Beau took a big gulp from his.

"I guess that's a no." Pop laughed.

CHAPTER ELEVEN

Beau

I STARED AT THE BOARD. Clare's ideas were about money and growth. Mine were the opposite. I'd seen how big orchards had lost touch with the essence of apple growing. They were there to fill the market and make as much of a profit as they could. It wasn't a bad philosophy. If they didn't follow it, they would fold.

My ideas could make money too but not on the same scale. I wanted to keep the family feel of the orchard. I wanted to bring something different to the area. What would Clare think, though? She'd probably think it was some idyllic venture that would never work. And the more I thought about it, the more I realised it probably wouldn't.

She'd put her ideas out there for me to see. I should afford her the same respect. Being judged was hard. Being judged by Clare was harder. But she'd already been judging me for days. It didn't make any difference if she criticised my ideas.

I should have spoken up when Nan and Pop offered us the opportunity to open up to each other. It would have been easier with them there. I wouldn't have felt the scrutiny of Clare's stare. They'd have helped guide the conversation. But no, I was a coward. Instead of opening up, I shut down.

Footsteps sounded along the corridor. Clare's footsteps. They were heavy but not the same way Dad's were heavy. Hers weren't heavy from size and weight but from determination.

I'd lost my opportunity to write my ideas on the board before she arrived. It would have been easier writing them down without her watching me.

"Good morning," Clare said as she walked in.

I swung my chair around and faced her. "Good morning."

Black fur clung to her t-shirt. From Clementine, I assumed.

"I see Clementine has left her mark on you this morning."

Clare's eyebrows drew together. I looked at her shirt, and her eyes followed. Shit, what if it wasn't from Clementine? What if Clementine was dead? Clare laughed and attempted to pat the fur off. I watched as her hands pressed down over her chest, each movement more persistent than the last.

"She was extra smoochy this morning."

"Does she still drool?" I turned my eyes away so I didn't drool. Clare's body was no longer that of a teenager. She was a woman and a damn hot one at that.

"Yes." Clare sat down.

That was exactly why she'd chosen Clementine. She

said no one else would want a black cat that drooled. She was unwanted. A misfit. Maybe that's why she'd chosen to be my friend.

Clare turned to the board. "Maybe we can talk about your ideas today."

I nodded even though she wasn't looking at me. "Mine don't really compare to yours."

"I think we should look at all of our options." Her voice was quiet, calm.

I took a deep breath. "My ideas aren't so much about growth but about diversity on a different scale."

She rolled her chair to the left. I mirrored her move. Was this what it was going to be like going forward? We'd stare at our own screens, hardly talking, but every now and then, we'd move to the side and have a conversation? We'd always had so much to say to each other, and now...we didn't.

"My idea has different levels." I took a breath. "We've lost so many of our apple varieties as our orchards have grown. Biodiversity has virtually disappeared. The first part of my idea centres on that, about bringing back some older varieties. Our apple trees here have a limited life. As we replant, I'd like to see them changed."

Clare stared openly at me. "Would there be a market for that?"

"I think so. How many times have you heard people say apples don't taste like they used to?"

"When I first started in the orchard, people would say it all the time. But that's dwindled."

"They say it because we're not growing for the best taste anymore. It's more about what's good to harvest, store and transport."

"So, you think these apples will be more popular?"

"Our apples are mainly sold in Tasmania. Dad has worked hard to keep our share of the market. Tasmania's food trail is growing in popularity; we're known for our gourmet foods. Bringing these old varieties back will give us an edge in that market, not only in fruit outlets but with local chefs."

She nodded. "And if we started to grow those varieties here, we could also add them to our nursery. But not on a commercial scale, more like a speciality product."

Her mind was working at warp speed like it always did. I was more confident knowing she was looking at all avenues. She was actually listening and considering my idea.

Her mouth twisted like it sometimes did when she was thinking. "And having different apples means more biodiversity, which means there's less threat from disease."

"Exactly."

"But is there a market? I know you said there is, but what evidence do you have?"

"In the States, there are people called Apple Detectives. They search for heirloom apple varieties. Orchardists grow and market them to consumers who are tired of the same old apples. It's not about serving the whole market; heirloom apples couldn't do that. It's about filling a niche market."

"So, we'd still need to grow our commercial varieties," she concluded. "We'd need to learn a hell of a lot about these old varieties. They became less popular for commercial orchards because they bruise easily, and they may not work well with our current storage and transport practices."

That was true. Our cool-room was a controlled

atmosphere. Sucking the oxygen out and keeping the temperature low slowed the ripening of apples.

"Yes, I think we'd need to do a lot of research to know which ones will fit best with how we operate. But because we sell locally, there will be less risk."

"You said your idea had other levels?"

OK, this was where I needed to sell the idea. "I think we should tap into the tourist industry."

"How?"

"Pick-your-own produce is becoming more popular. I was thinking of making it a whole experience, starting with making their own apple boxes, then picking their own fruit and maybe even juicing some apples. The apples that normally go to waste because of colour, shape or size can be juiced instead. Ninety-nine per cent of our apples would be used."

Clare didn't look convinced. "And you think there's money in this?"

"You don't pay pickers, packers, storage and transport, so there are savings to be had."

"There would still be increased costs."

"Yes, that's something we need to consider. And we'd still need the commercial crop and the costs associated with that, just reduced."

She grabbed the marker and went to the board. My eyes drifted down to her butt. Yep, she'd filled out in more than one place. I longed to touch her in all those places, to kiss her in all of those places. I licked my lips. These thoughts were not helping. I needed to get back to the subject at hand.

"Remember how we'd make and repair apple crates for pocket money?" I asked her. "We'd race each other, and Pop would sometimes make us start all over again if our work was sloppy? I want our kids to experience that too. I want to keep the family feel of the farm."

What the hell did I just say? I watched Clare for her reaction— the marker paused for the briefest moment before she continued writing. She added heirloom apples and pick-your-own produce to the board.

Clare's phone rang. She fished it out of her pocket as she put the marker down.

"Hello."

I turned back to my desk. I closed my eyes and took a breath. My ideas were out there. What did she think of them?

"OK. I'll be there in a minute."

She hung up the phone and grabbed her keys off the desk.

"I need to go. One of the tractors is shagged."

I stood up. "Can I help with something?"

"No thanks," she said as she hurried out the door.

She'd shut me down in a microsecond. She didn't even consider the question. How could I prove my worth if she didn't give me a chance?

"WHOA, slow down, cowboy. You said what?" Mike, my mental health support person of seven years, asked. He wasn't just my support person anymore; he was my friend. At first, when I'd lived in Victoria, we'd meet in person at a men's group. We'd see each other at the weekly meet-ups and go for coffee afterwards. Back then, it had been all about my mental health. But over the years, when I'd moved overseas, we'd developed a deeper and stronger friendship. We spoke on a different level. He told me what I needed to hear. He no longer led me gently to an answer. He didn't beat around the bush.

"I didn't mean it like that. It just came out."

He raised his eyebrows. "Your future children just came out, just like that. What did Clare have to say?"

"Surprisingly, nothing. The whiteboard marker paused for a moment. Then she continued writing, and not one word was mentioned."

"Mmmm...OK. Maybe she thought about how you were once a family but weren't anymore. Maybe she wasn't thinking about your progeny." He rubbed his chin. "You know there are a million steps you need to work through before you can bring up children or a relationship or anything remotely romantic."

I sighed and sat on my bed. "It just slipped out."

I'd been obsessing over the slip-up all afternoon. I was grateful Clare didn't say anything. Maybe she thought nothing of it. I could have meant children with other partners, not each other. Just because she didn't have a partner now, it didn't mean anything.

My big mouth could have made her turn against me. I'd watched for a change in her attitude all day. It didn't change from cold to Antarctic, at least.

I'd been so concerned I'd forgotten to tell her about how I wanted to implement beehives of our own on the farm. I'd seen how much of a difference it had made elsewhere. My overthinking had stopped me.

"OK. I'll give you the benefit of the doubt. Tell me about your parents."

"They're good. They're really excited to have me home."

"And how do you feel about that? Is it overwhelming?"

"They haven't been pushing me. We sort of have surface conversations."

"Are you ready to have any other sort of conversation?"

"I did try to say something about joining the gym because it's good for mental health. All I heard was crickets."

Mike nodded. "I suppose that was disappointing."

"I've waited a long time to speak to them about my illness." I shrugged. It was frustrating, but what could I do? "I guess it can wait a little while longer."

"It's hard to say those first few words."

"Was it hard for you?" I asked.

"Hell yeah." Mike laughed.

Lisa, his wife, came to the camera. "It was torture. I'd ask, he'd say nothing. I'd ask again. Nothing. But I had to be patient. I knew he had to be ready."

"Lisa, patient. Can you imagine?" Mike said.

She slapped him over the head and walked away. I grinned. They cracked me up.

"Dad has got me working with Clare to make the orchard more sustainable."

"And how's that going?"

"She wasn't happy about us working together at first. Maybe she still isn't, but it's less noticeable."

She'd been consumed with the tractor problem for the rest of the morning. And then she rushed off to another meeting she told me nothing about. I was going to have to be more forceful if I was going to be a part of the Hart Apples team.

"Just surface conversations with her too?"

"Yeah."

"And what do you think about that?"

"I think it's safe."

Lisa giggled in the background. "So, you can talk about your unborn children but not about your past?"

Mike rolled his eyes, but the way he was holding in his smile told me he agreed with her. "And do you think safe is going to help you?"

"No, but I'm not ready to move out of safe mode yet. I don't think I have the right to ask her forgiveness." I sighed. I wasn't sure I'd ever be ready.

"Do you think you're not worthy?"

"I don't know. I mean, I know I am worthy. That's why I came back. But at the same time, I'm not. I hurt her. And I know I need to talk to her to ask her forgiveness and open up so she can see me again, below the skin, but I'm not strong enough if she doesn't like what she sees."

"Do you like what you see?"

"Most of the time."

I looked away from the camera and stared at the wall. There was nothing there but blank plaster, but it was better than seeing Mike's expression.

"Why do you think she won't like what she sees? She liked you well enough before."

"Before I let her down."

"Are you talking about the kiss or not calling her?"

"Both."

"You need to talk to her about it."

"I know. Nan and Pop seem to think she has the capacity to forgive me."

"Now you need to believe it too."

He was right. I didn't only come back for my parents and the orchard. I came back for Clare.

"No more next-generation talk until you sort your shit out."

I groaned. "It just slipped out."

"Nothing really *just* slips out."

"Yeah. OK."

"And stop thinking about kissing her."

With that, he hung up.

He sure was asking a lot of me.

CHAPTER TWELVE

Clare

If nothing else, Beau was persistent. When I received another call about the tractor, instead of asking me if I needed help, he followed me straight out. Now we were standing beside each other, staring at it.

Pete looked between us, a crease on his forehead. "It was working good this morning. After morning tea, nothing."

"How long has it been playing up?" Beau asked.

"Since before the last week."

"Since that call two weeks ago, then." Beau walked around the tractor, rubbing the back of his neck. He turned to me. "What did you do last time to get it started?"

"We didn't need to do anything. It started on its own," I said.

"Did the mechanic look at it?"

I shook my head. I'd been too bloody distracted by Beau. I wasn't thinking straight with him here. My mind was drawn to him. My body was drawn to him. Then there were the business ideas that kept rolling around my head. He was the cause of those too. Everything was status quo before he came.

"Can you try turning it on for me?" Beau asked Pete.

Pete nodded and hopped onto the tractor. He turned the key. Nothing happened.

"Could be a fuel block," Beau said. I walked around to the other side of the tractor while Beau examined the motor. He pointed to the half-empty fuel bowl. I nodded. Pete hopped down and joined us, staring at the motor. I had the impression that it was just a chunk of metal to him.

Beau stepped forward and touched the fuel bowl. "See the fuel? It should be at the top. Either there's air in the line or there's a blockage."

"What do we do?" Pete asked.

"We need to figure out which one it is first. But not here, in the middle of the orchard. We don't want an accidental spill."

"I'll call a foreman to organise a tow," I said.

I walked a few metres away and made the call. All the while, I watched while Beau and Pete talked to each other, smiling. After the call, I wanted to join them. But that felt dangerous. But why? Why couldn't I just have a normal conversation with two people? Because Beau wasn't any normal person. His effect on me wasn't normal. If it was, I wouldn't have missed calling the mechanic two weeks ago. Me forgetting to do that would be another point in Beau's favour if it got out.

"I'm going to head to the shed to get everything ready," I said to them.

"Always so efficient," Beau said.

Was he having a dig at me?

"I don't want the tractor to be out of action any longer than it needs to be."

I left them standing there. It wouldn't have been out of action if I'd had my act together. I couldn't do anything about the past, but I could make up for it now. I strode to the shed and started pulling out everything Beau would need to fix the problem—tools, buckets, air compressor.

Memories crept in. One of my most vivid from when we were young children.

BEAU and I ran as the storm raged through the orchard. The ferocious wind was all around us. Branches were blown almost vertical. The rain stung our skin and soaked our clothes. Sticks, rocks and dust lashed at our bare legs. Branches flew around, and ladders crashed to the ground. We covered our heads with our arms protecting ourselves from flying objects.

"We need to find shelter," Beau yelled above the wind.

He led me up a row of apples towards an abandoned tractor. We huddled underneath.

"We need to move to the back wheel," Beau shouted. "There will be more protection there."

My eyes were squeezed shut. Beau grabbed my hand and yanked me backwards. He shoved me against the wheel and put his arms around me. The hail pelted against the tractor. The thunder was so close the ground shook. The sound was deafening. Beau was shaking against me but never once let me go. Not until the storm had passed.

When I opened my eyes, I turned to Beau. His face was covered in blood from a gash in his head. He wiped his face and glanced at his hand. Without a second thought of himself, he examined me closely and asked if I was OK.

. . .

VOICES PULLED me out of my memory. I rubbed my arms and the goosebumps that had settled there. Before Beau and Pete pulled into the shed, I checked I had everything they needed.

It was my fault we were out in the orchard that day. We were told a big storm was coming and to stay inside. But I wanted to go to the tree house. Six-year-old me thought the storm would be more fun there. When we were getting yelled at by our parents because we could have been killed, Beau never once said I was to blame. Would he do the same today if the tractor breakdown came up with his dad?

Beau took Pete through the motions of figuring out the problem. If Pete didn't understand something, Beau took his time explaining it to him. Then when they discovered it was a blockage, he showed him how to fix it. These skills were good for Pete to learn and could easily be transferred back to his home when he returned.

"That should fix the problem for now," Beau said to Pete. "Once we get through the busy part of the season, I can show you how to drain and clean the tank."

Pete gave him a toothy smile. "Thanks, Boss."

What the fuck? Boss? He'd only been here a few weeks, and he was boss? I'd been here for years and was the actual boss, but he still called me Miss Clare.

After Pete drove off, Beau came over to help me clean up. Not only did he have everyone chatting and smiling, but now he had proven himself in the mechanic department too. And in the clean-up department. The man was insufferable.

"HEARD YOU FIXED A TRACTOR PROBLEM TODAY?" Justin said from the doorway.

"Just a small fuel problem. It was an easy fix."

I stared at my computer screen. I didn't want to engage in this conversation. I should be more grateful that he fixed the problem. If it had been anyone else, I would have been. Why couldn't I afford Beau the same respect? Because it was Beau. And I was being petty.

I took a deep breath and directed my attention to Beau and Justin. "Beau figured out the problem straight away. It saved us a lot of time."

Beau's eyes widened.

"Great. Time and money are everything on a farm. Good job." Justin gave Beau a smile before he left.

"Thank you," Beau said when we were alone.

I shrugged. "Got to give credit where credit is due."

It was a big thing for Beau to be acknowledged by his father. There had been very little of that when we were growing up, like that time he fixed the sprinkler system.

BEAU TURNED on the sprinkler system, but nothing happened. Not one drop of water came out. We looked at each other. We needed to get it going. His dad had told us to, and we knew better than to not do what we were told.

"We'll need to check the hoses and connections," Beau said as he walked to the quad bike.

I followed and hopped on behind him.

We rode slowly, checking the hoses as we went. There were no gushing leaks from a broken connection, no spraying water from a hole in the hose.

One of the foremen called out to us, and we headed over

to him. He held his hat in his hand as he wiped the sweat and dirt from his brow. "What're you kids doing?"

"The sprinklers aren't working," Beau said.

He nodded. "I'll get someone onto it."

"We've checked most of the hoses. It all looks good. We're going to check out the water pump."

"OK. I'll get Simon to meet you there."

Beau and I rode to the pump. Beau set straight to work, and after some troubleshooting, he found that the strainer was blocked. He started working on it. By the time Simon arrived, Beau had sorted the problem.

Simon gave him a clap on the back. "Good job, kid." Then he got on the two-way. "Beau has sorted the problem. Can you turn a sprinkler on and see if it works?"

We waited in anticipation.

"Yep, they're working now," someone called over the two-way.

Simon gave us a big smile. "Thanks. You saved us a lot of time."

Beau nodded.

When we got back, Justin didn't acknowledge what Beau had done. He would have known. From all the thumbs up we got as we rode back to the workshop, the whole farm knew. I saw how downtrodden ten-year-old Beau looked. He only wanted to be recognised for doing something good.

THERE WERE SO many instances over our childhood that had added up, that had made him feel that this wasn't the place for him. And to come back here and try to fit in after being away for so long must have been hard for him. I often wondered what it was like for him at home now. He didn't talk about it. And there was no way I was going to ask. We needed to keep this professional. And not just because my job relied on it.

I needed to keep it about business because a part of me still cared about Beau, a little too much. I wanted to know about this new Beau. I wanted to share things with him. But getting close to him was dangerous. For my job and for my heart.

CHAPTER THIRTEEN

Beau

I STOOD UP. "I'm heading down to the nursery."

Clare's eyes narrowed. "What for?"

"I thought I'd like to get a better look at where the magic happens."

I walked to the door. One. Two. Th—

"I'll come down with you," Clare said.

"OK."

I knew she wouldn't be able to resist.

She'd been her same distant self, even after I'd helped with the tractor a month ago. I'd hoped that it would have put a crack in that tough exterior of hers, but I don't think it even scratched the surface.

We walked in silence. When we reached the nursery, a smiling lady came out of the office to meet us. Energy oozed out of her. She looked familiar.

"Charli is our nursery supervisor," Clare said to me. "Charli, this is Beau."

"Oooh, the infamous Beau has finally come to visit little old me." She took my hand and gave it a friendly shake.

Clare set her feet apart. To anyone else, it would have looked like a natural stance. But I knew it was the equivalent of someone stiffening their shoulders.

"Have we met before? You look familiar," I said.

Charli shook her head and rolled her eyes. "Beau Hart, we went to the same school." She laughed. "But you only had eyes for Clare. The rest of us were just background noise."

I nearly choked.

"You weren't missing much," Clare said to Charli, her face as red as an apple.

Charli didn't miss a beat. "I'm sure Clare has told you all about the nursery. It's really grown over the last few years. Just today, I prepared a big order for a nursery on the mainland." She led me over to some youngstock. "These are all waiting to be picked up."

There were probably forty trees. "All for one nursery?"

"Oh yeah, sometimes I wonder if we'll be able to grow them fast enough."

Clare had built this nursery from nothing. To grow that many trees ahead of time took confidence in a growing market.

"How did you know all of this was needed?" I asked, waving my hand around.

Clare shrugged. "Intuition."

"Don't be so blasé," Charli said.

Clare sighed. "The popularity of growing your own food has increased steadily in the last ten years. There are over 60,000 hobby farms in Australia, and the number keeps growing."

"How'd you figure that out?"

"I watched the news."

I'd recognise that smart-arse tone anywhere.

"Tell me more about the operation," I said to Charli.

She glanced at Clare.

"You go right ahead," Clare said and turned on her heel, marching to the office.

"Are you two having a lovers' tiff?" Charli asked.

Jeez, she was forward. Maybe she was one of those people who had no filter.

"For the past two months."

Charli nodded. "So, since you got back then."

"The moment I walked through the door." I looked back towards the nursery office. "Probably before that, if we're being honest."

"Probably."

We walked around the nursery while Charli explained everything to me. What Clare had created here was incredible. I would never be able to measure up to her. Dad thinking I'd done a good job with the tractor paled in comparison, like comparing an ant to a dinosaur. This...this was an enterprise all of its own.

Clare didn't need to come up with any ideas to future-proof the business. She'd already done it with the nursery. Surely Dad knew that. Everything she'd done, including the international workers, was all the business needed. My contribution was just whitewash. I couldn't compete.

But I didn't want to compete. I wanted to earn her trust back. I wanted to build something with her. The problem was I felt like I was competing with her to earn Dad's respect. To be accepted by him.

I needed to separate the two.

"Well, lover boy, you've seen everything now," Charli said as we approached the office.

"Thanks for showing me around."

"My pleasure."

Clare was waiting outside the office. She lifted her eyes skyward.

"It could have been your pleasure too, if you'd joined us," I said.

"You and pleasure, not sure that's a perfect match," Clare said as she walked away.

Charli nudged me in the ribs and inclined her chin towards Clare.

I started to follow.

"And what do you think is a perfect match for me?"

"Clare," Charli called out and laughed.

I turned and gave her a grin. Nothing like having someone on my side. Clare gave her the finger.

"A rainbow bee-eater," Clare said over her shoulder.

She thought the perfect match for me was a bird?

"You're beautiful but deadly."

Interesting analogy. I quickened my pace. "Beautiful?"

"That's the thing you latched onto?"

"It was better than deadly." I caught up to her.

"You reckon? Beauty is often dangerous."

"So you're saying I'm dangerous?"

Memories of our younger days and our fun banter made me smile.

I STARTED to gather the ingredients for dinner. Cooking was a favourite pastime. When I was in Italy working on a family orchard, I learnt a lot about cooking from Nonna. She was little and round and always happy. She came alive when we cooked together—laughing, clapping and joking.

Often it became a family affair with three generations in the kitchen.

In California, we took turns cooking meals. The kitchen was industrial, all stainless steel. We would stand around, talking and offering help to the cook when needed. I could have cooked and eaten in my manager's quarters, but there was no fun in that. You learnt a lot about your fellow workers when you spent time with them in such a family-oriented setting.

"Do you want some help?" Mum asked as she put her apron on.

"Sure, you can peel the potatoes for the gnocchi if you like."

I'd tried to think about what Mum and Dad would like to eat for dinner. They were not what I would call adventurous eaters. It was usually meat and three veg. Sometimes, they would buy something from the Chinese restaurant in town or have a pizza. But it was rare. I'd chosen gnocchi because it was potato-based, and everyone liked potatoes.

"How many potatoes?" she asked.

"These ones here." I pointed to the ones I'd placed on the bench.

"Will this be enough?"

"Yes, this is plenty for the three of us. I'm making a tomato sauce to go with it."

"Your dad doesn't like rich food."

"I won't make it too rich."

"What about meat? Dad will want some meat."

I held in a sigh. "I'm making arrosticini as well. It's lamb on a skewer."

"OK."

She stood beside me and peeled.

The silence was killing me. "In Italy, we'd cook the potatoes and then peel them before making the gnocchi."

"It's much easier to peel before you cook," Mum said.

I nodded. There was nothing else to say. I mean, the Italians had been doing it for 200 years, but what would they know? I pulled the lamb out of the fridge and started dicing it.

Mum paused her peeling. "Should you prepare the tomato sauce first?"

"I can make the sauce when the gnocchi are resting."

"It needs to rest?"

"Yes. First, we need to cook the potato, and then we mix it with flour, salt and eggs. Next, we make the gnocchi and let it rest before we cook it."

"It would be easier to just make potatoes."

I clenched my teeth. I wasn't asking her to make the gnocchi.

Cooking was all about creating and getting flavour into the food. Even the simplest ingredients could become a mouth-watering meal. But it wasn't just about the food or ingredients. It was about the love that went into preparing it and the joy of sharing the food together.

We worked side by side, not saying much to each other. Dad came in as I put a pot of water on the stove for the gnocchi.

"Just in time, Justin. Beau is making us Italian food for dinner," Mum said from the sink where she was washing dishes.

Dad glanced at the gnocchi. He nodded and went to the table.

"The lamb is a starter. It comes from Abruzzo and is a dish the local shepherds enjoyed," I said.

"Did you live near Abruzzo?" Mum asked as she wiped her hands on a towel.

"No. The dish is eaten in many other provinces now. It was easy for us to cook after a long day out in the orchard."

I started threading the lamb onto the skewers I'd soaked. Dad would be impatient to start his meal. "This will only take a couple of minutes to cook."

Mum was still hovering in the kitchen. "You can sit down, Mum. I'll bring them over when they're ready."

She wiped her hands on the towel again as if unsure. She gave a small nod and joined Dad at the table. I grilled the lamb and took it out to the table for us to share. Dad picked a skewer up and examined it before putting it on his plate.

I grabbed a piece of crusty bread. "Usually, we would use the bread to soak the juices up from the lamb. Then we would have bread that's full of flavour too."

I showed them what I meant. Mum was hesitant but did as I did.

"Heard you and Clare went out to the nursery today," Dad said as he took a piece of bread and took a bite out of it. He didn't soak up the lamb juices.

"Yes, Charli showed me around."

"Clare built that nursery up from nothing. Quite ingenious," he said.

As if I didn't already know that. "Yes, it's quite the operation."

Dad nodded and ate some of the lamb.

"No more problems with the tractor?" he asked.

Looks like it was going to be another work discussion at the dinner table.

"No. If it happens again, we'll have to drain the tank and sort it once and for all."

He nodded.

"How's Clare?" Mum asked. "I haven't had time to chat with her lately."

"Good. She keeps a tight rein on things. Always knows what's happening," I said.

"As a good manager should," Dad replied.

Would he think of me as a good manager one day? I had a lot of catching up to do where Clare was concerned. And I'm sure he was well aware of it. This wasn't the first time he'd pointed out her superiority.

He finished his arrosticini and pushed the plate away. I guess the fact that he ate it all was positive. He must have liked it.

"That was delicious, Beau," Mum said in an overly bright voice.

Dad's reaction was exactly the same as when we had to do a science project at high school. I'd chosen to do it about bees. I did a diorama of our orchard and placed beehives in strategic places. I explained on little cards why I had chosen these places based on scientific evidence. I also showed places where fresh water should be accessible to bees, including wood for a landing pad and a way for the bees to get out if they fell in the water. It went into a lot of detail, including noise reduction and when to spray pesticides.

My project was in the top three and was displayed on an awards night. The teacher led my parents to my project. She was gushing about the detail and how much effort I put in. She explained how this type of environmental science would change the world in years to come. It was the future the world needed to become more sustainable.

Dad nodded when she finished speaking, took another look at my project and walked away. Mum squeezed my shoulders, gave me a big smile, and said 'good work' before following him.

I hid my tears from my teacher. Here was someone I respected, telling my parents my way of thinking was the future, and they didn't care. They didn't care about me or what I thought.

Later, when we sat together for the awards, Mum leant over and said, 'Dad thought your project was good too.' As if those few words made up for his dismissal. Like it was OK for him to treat me like that.

From that point on, the only thing I cared about was getting away.

CHAPTER FOURTEEN

Clare

Beau was waiting for me outside the shed. His face lit up into a smile as soon as I opened the car door. That bloody smile was a trap. And I fell into it every time.

Beau handed me a coffee. "Ready for our morning rounds?"

"Sure am. Thanks for the coffee."

This had been our routine for the past few weeks. We'd walk through a different part of the orchard every day. We'd examine the waste on the ground, the apples on the trees and what the pickers were doing. The pickers would continue their work around us unless we stopped to ask them a question.

We'd check out the packing shed. It was good to see how the sorting was going and to check what apples were being rejected. We then fed this information back to the foremen. Beau had taken over that task, and he enjoyed the teaching opportunity. He'd taken over many tasks. I'd shut him down time and again, but he was persistent. He'd always offer to help, but I said I didn't need any help. After that, he became insistent and suggested where he could help. He wore me down.

We'd then look at the storage shed and marvel at how it was filling up. I loved how every day, more and more space was filled. Even though the storage shed was huge, the empty floor space was disappearing.

We strolled past the workshop, the place Beau and I'd repaired crates as kids. Sometimes we'd become bored with hammering the two-inch nails into the rough wood, and we'd hop into the crates and eat fresh apples, the crunch of our bites echoing through the shed. Other times the pounding rain hitting the tin roof would drown out our hammer falls.

As we walked, Beau took the lid off his cup and tipped it back.

"Surely you're not that desperate for that last bit of caffeine," I said.

"It's not the caffeine. It's the sweet, frothy milk."

He turned to me with a milk moustache.

"I think it's supposed to go in your mouth." I reached out and ran my thumb across his lips, gathering up the remnants of froth. I brought my thumb to my mouth and licked the froth off. Beau watched me with such intensity I forgot where I was. My mind rushed back to the day he left. How he'd studied my face, his eyes roaming everywhere before his lips met mine in a fervour.

"Taste good?" Beau asked.

I stepped away from him, my heart beating fast. I laughed and pushed the memory away. "As sweet as fresh honey."

"Speaking of honey, I've been talking to Pop, and he thinks it's a good idea to add bees and honey to my idea."

"Pop said that?"

"Hi, Beau," a female voice called out. I looked in the direction it came from. A blonde woman was up a ladder waving at Beau. I'm sure she had plenty of apples to pick but, for some reason, needed to call out to Beau. I gritted my teeth.

Beau waved back and gave a smile.

"Finished socialising?" I asked him.

"Would you rather me be rude?"

"I'd rather her do her work."

Beau shook his head but didn't wipe the stupid smile off his face. I was glad he found it amusing.

I didn't want to talk about her anymore. "Pop said you should add bees to your idea?"

"Yeah. Bees are good for the orchard, right? We can't have apples if we don't have bees."

If Pop was getting in on his idea, I could be in trouble. He may be retired, but he was still an influence. And if we went with Beau's idea, would there be room enough for both of us? I turned my attention to the trees beside us, pretending to examine the apples.

"Pop said if we're going to go with heirloom apples, we need to remember that the flowers need to be the same colour because bees like to stick to one type of blossom. I'd forgotten about that."

Pop was always the logical one.

"Then he said it would be good if we produced honey as well, to keep with the theme of biodiversity."

Of course he did.

What was I supposed to say? I didn't want to diminish

Beau's excitement. Resigned, I said, "I guess that makes sense. Without bees, many ecosystems would cease to exist."

Beau turned to me; his energy was like a magnet. He held my full attention. "We could do our part to help prevent a pollination crisis. And create a new avenue for education."

The pollination crisis was a real thing. Intensive farming needed bees. And I didn't just mean a couple of hives. We had hives transported in at precisely the right time every season for bees to pollinate the trees. Nearly two-thirds of the world's agricultural production depended on bees. But it was also intensive farming that was detrimental to them—destruction of habitat, pesticides and climate change. All caused a reduction in their population.

"And what exactly do you and Pop propose?"

POP WAS SITTING under the tree, watching the bees. His eyes and head followed their path. I parked my car in the driveway.

Nan poked her head out of the kitchen window. "Hi, love."

"Hi, Nan." That was all the words I could afford her. I marched over to Pop.

"Whose side are you on?" I stood in front of him, my hands on my hips.

"Pardon?" He gave me a smile with his eyebrows raised.

"You know exactly what I'm talking about. Planting ideas in Beau's head about including bees in his plan."

Pop looked at the beehive. It was late afternoon, and the

bee activity was dying down for the day. Often, we'd sit here, listening to the bees together. Their constant buzzing drowned out our thoughts and emotions. I'm sure that's one of the reasons Pop loved it out here so much.

"When the area was full of apple orchards, all we could smell was the scent of apple blossoms, and with that, we heard the constant buzzing of bees. Sadly, not anymore."

"Don't try to deflect my question." I stood firm, glaring at him.

"Are you coming in for a cuppa?" Nan called out.

"No," I shouted.

"Yes," Pop replied, ignoring my response.

I grunted and turned on my heel. I wanted to march right back to the house, but I was aware that Pop's legs wouldn't be able to keep up with my angry pace. I slowed down for him.

Before Pop could sit at the table, I said again, "Whose side are you on?"

"The bees."

I gritted my teeth and took a deep breath.

"You know damn well what I mean. Why are you putting ideas in Beau's head?" I sat down opposite Pop.

"I didn't put it in his head. It was already there. He just hadn't told you about it. All I did was encourage him."

"What about my ideas? Why would you help him and not me?"

Nan brought the cups to the table. "Clare darling, this isn't about you and Beau. This is about the orchard."

"And the bees."

"So, you think his ideas are better?"

"No one said that," Nan said as she sat down.

"I've worked hard for the business for seven years. I've

always done what's best for it. And now he's going to take it away."

I shut up before I said too much. Nan and Pop looked at each other, again with the silent conversation.

"And then he'll leave? Is that what you were going to add?" Nan asked.

I shrugged.

Nan came over to my side of the table and took my hand. "Your mum died when you were such a delicate age, you were still a child, and you took on so much of the burden yourself. You helped raise your sister. You supported your father beyond measure." She reached her hand out and stroked my hair. It was something Mum had done when I was young. My shoulder muscles relaxed. "And then Beau left. The two people you loved most in the world were gone."

My throat tightened, and she put her arm around my shoulder.

"Are you worried about losing your job or losing Beau?"

My chest constricted as a tear rolled down my cheek. I couldn't answer. Both would be heartbreaking. But one would ruin me.

"Beau to you is like sugar to a bee," Pop said. "Since he's been back, we've seen more emotion from you than we've seen in years."

Nan laughed and patted my hand. "My gosh, yes. Happiness, frustration, jealousy."

"I'm not jealous." I pulled my hand away.

"Right, so you don't mind all those girls paying him so much attention?" Pop laughed.

"It's annoying, that's all. We've got better things to do."

"And him talking to Pop doesn't make you jealous?" Nan said, poking me in the side.

How was I going to answer that without sounding petty? I'd already accused Pop of taking his side.

"No."

Pop laughed so hard he cried. He slapped his leg and declared, "You're so full of shit, girl."

I shook my head, willing my smile away. "And he doesn't make me happy."

CHAPTER FIFTEEN

Beau

Me: *I need your help.*

Almost immediately, I got a reply from Clare: *With what?*

Me: *I saw a puppy on the side of the road. When I got out to catch it, it ran off.*

Clare: *Where are you?*

Me: *A couple of km from work*

Clare: *I'll be there soon.*

I reread the messages and smiled. She was one of the only people I knew who used correct grammar and punctuation in a text message. I paced the side of the road. There was no sign of the puppy.

Clare hadn't hesitated when I'd asked for help. Months ago, it would have been different. Then, I wouldn't have been surprised if she'd added more fuel to the fire if I was burning alive. The barriers were falling like branches when we thinned apple trees.

Where was Clare? It had been ten minutes already.

At last, the sound of her ute approached. She pulled up behind my car and hopped out with a handful of things—a bottle of water, a bowl and what looked like meat in Ziplock bags. Smart thinking.

"Where'd you see this puppy?"

"It was back there a bit."

"Are you sure it was a puppy?" she asked as she walked to where I'd pointed. She stood on the edge of the road and scanned the paddock and trees beyond.

"It looked like a puppy or small dog."

"Have a bag of meat. Open it up so it can smell it."

I took one of the bags. "It could be anywhere by now."

"Maybe, maybe not. He could be watching us, seeing what we're doing."

I guess she was right. Dogs were smart and curious, even as curious as a cat.

"Let's head out in a V shape. Go slow, stop and call. If there's no sign, keep walking."

We separated and took it slow. Every time I stopped, I listened and looked for movement. But there was nothing, not even wind rustling the grass. I glanced over at Clare. She was watching me. I kept walking.

Thirty minutes in, I was sure Clare would call it. We'd been wandering around without any indication that the creature was still there, but there was no sign that Clare wanted to leave. She was still moving slowly, examining the area. I couldn't give up. That poor puppy would be out here, alone and scared. We needed to keep going.

A flash of white stopped me in my tracks. Clare turned, and I pointed. The puppy, dog or whatever it was, was halfway between us. We approached it slowly.

"Hey puppy, what're you doing out here?" I asked in a low voice.

It stayed stock still, watching us.

"It's OK, baby, we won't hurt you," Clare said in a soothing voice.

The puppy sat and watched. As I got closer, I could see it was some sort of terrier with grey and wiry white fur. When Clare and I reached each other, we crouched down.

"Come here, sweetie." Clare held out a piece of meat. The puppy didn't budge.

"We've got some food for you." I held out a piece of meat. The pup's head tilted.

The three of us sat and looked at each other. This could take a while. At least, I hadn't imagined seeing the pup. I tilted backwards until my butt hit the ground. Clare followed suit. I leant forward and placed a cube of meat on the ground. Not too close. I didn't want the puppy to get scared.

"Thanks for coming to help me."

"You'd do the same for me."

I'd do anything for her.

"I wonder how long it's been out here for," I said.

"Its fur is dirty, and it's quite skinny."

The puppy took a couple of timid steps forward.

"Good boy or girl. Good puppy," I said, encouraging it.

Clare put water in the bowl and reached forward to place it on the ground. The puppy took a step back.

"How are we going to catch it?" I asked.

"No idea."

The puppy stepped forward again. Its nose twitched.

"Good idea to bring meat."

"It was Nan's idea. I dropped in there on the way."

I nodded. Clare was lucky to have her nan and pop. Even though mine lived in town, we weren't that close. They hadn't really made an effort when I was younger.

Maybe because I didn't talk much, and they found me awkward. I didn't have that problem with Nan and Pop, though. They'd always included me, whether I was having a talkative day or not. When I was away, I sent them postcards and updates every week.

I kept my eye on the puppy as it took another step forward.

"Do you like being back?" Clare asked. My skin tingled. It was the most personal thing she'd asked me in the months I'd been home.

"Yes. It's not how I remember it. It's different."

"Do you feel different?"

"Sometimes. Sometimes I worry about what Mum and Dad are thinking. I don't want to disappoint them."

I didn't want to disappoint Clare either. This thing with the future of the business stressed me out. It was a huge responsibility, and what if we got it wrong? I had a lot to prove, and I wondered if this was some sort of test that I was sure to fail. My ideas wouldn't be good enough, and Dad was trying to show me that without saying it. My anxiety was talking again.

But in some ways, I knew there was truth in my thoughts. I could never measure up to Clare in his eyes. He'd virtually said as much when he'd seen Clare's ideas on the board. Of course they were hers because they were good. That meant mine wouldn't be good in his eyes.

The puppy lunged and grabbed onto the meat. It chewed vigorously, grunting. While it was eating with such intensity, I reached out with another piece. It stopped chewing and watched my hand. As soon as I let the meat go and pulled my hand back, it resumed chewing.

"I know now that it's more the expectations I have for

myself rather than their expectations. When I worry, I need to talk myself around."

Clare nodded in my peripheral vision.

"I like spending time with you." I risked a glance at her. What would she say? Would she brush it off? Maybe she'd ignore it and pay attention to the puppy instead. I just needed something positive, something to help me feel that all was not lost. I rubbed my hand on my leg.

"Same." Her voice was quiet, unsure.

My chest felt light, like a crate of apples had been crushing it and the crate was lifted. Like when we'd covered ourselves in bags of apples as kids to see how many we could endure. I beat her by one bag.

The puppy barked. The piece of meat was gone. It wanted another. I put the meat closer this time, between Clare and me. This would be a big test. The puppy didn't hesitate. It went straight for it.

"We don't want to give him too much. It might give him a tummy ache," Clare said.

She reached out her hand to touch it. The puppy stopped chewing but didn't shy away and didn't growl.

"One more and I'll try to pick it up," I said.

She nodded. I held a piece of meat out and moved it closer to me so I could reach the puppy easier. When he was close, I picked him up and fed him.

"He must have been someone's puppy once. A wild dog wouldn't let you do that."

I held the puppy in my lap.

"What do we do now?" she asked.

"Take him home and give him a bath. Then put a post on social media, I guess."

"You can't take him back to your place. Your mum's allergic."

Shit. I'd forgotten.

"We'll take him to my place. He can stay until we find his home."

"And if we don't?"

"We'll re-evaluate then."

I gave the puppy another piece of meat. He ate it and then scratched and scratched and scratched.

"He's got fleas," I observed.

"We'll take my car and get some flea wash on the way home."

WE PULLED into a carport next to a weatherboard house. I hopped out of Clare's car and took in the view of the river and hills in the distance.

"Your view is fantastic," I said as I followed her to the back door.

"I was lucky to buy the house a few years ago before prices started rising." She unlocked the door to the laundry.

She'd bought a house, on her own, in her early twenties. All I had was the car I'd bought when I got home and some savings. She outclassed me in every way.

"I don't think the laundry tub will work well. It'll be too hard for the two of us to work together."

She was right. The tub was in the corner. We wouldn't be able to stand side by side without crushing each other. We walked down the hallway to a modern bathroom with a free-standing bath. The puppy was still in my arms. He, we'd confirmed he was a he, had barely moved since we'd got in the car. He'd slept for most of the drive.

"I'll grab some towels," Clare said.

"Good idea."

I scratched the puppy's ear. He leant into my hand, nuzzling it. I heard a sound behind me, expecting Clare. Instead, I found Clementine sitting in the doorway, her fluffy black fur sticking out in all directions.

"Clementine."

She sat and stared. I knelt down with the puppy in my arms.

"Come here, girl."

She considered me, and then the puppy, turned her nose into the air and walked away. Clare came in with towels and turned the bath on.

"Clementine still looks like she had a bad hair day," I said.

Clare looked around. "Was she here? She doesn't normally say hello to anyone."

"She left when she saw the puppy."

Clare placed a towel on the bottom of the bath and folded it in half. "It will make him feel more secure. He won't like it if his feet slip out from under him."

"OK."

"You learn these things when you have a cat who has bad hair days."

"You wash Clementine?" I laughed, imagining a soaked cat.

"Not anymore. I thought it would help tame her wild locks. It didn't."

Clare turned off the water and tested the warmth. I took the puppy over and lowered him into the water. He started scrambling straight away. What dog didn't like water?

"It's alright, little man, we're going to make you all clean," I said.

Clare poured water over him, wetting his fur. He

continued to scramble. Water was going everywhere. Clare used her arm to wipe her eyes. She was laughing.

"You need to hold him tighter," she told me.

"I don't want to hurt him."

She grabbed the shampoo bottle. It made a loud splutter as she squeezed it. The puppy slipped out of my hands and leapt out of the bath. His feet found no purchase on the tiles, and they slid in and out like he was doing some sort of weird dance. He headed for the door in awkward slow motion.

"Oh no, you don't," Clare exclaimed, launching herself at him and pinning him to the ground. I raced to close the door while Clare wrestled with the slippery dog. She clutched him to her chest and spoke to him in low tones.

"He likes his ear being scratched," I told her.

His frantic movements stopped, and she brought him back to the bath. Her t-shirt was soaking.

"We're going to need to talk to him the whole time," Clare said, "to keep him calm."

She placed him back in the bath, patting him and talking to him. I shook the shampoo bottle to make sure the liquid was at the top and squirted some in my hand. We continued talking while washing him, telling him he was a good boy and that it was nearly over.

"We need fresh water to rinse him," Clare said. The water was a murky grey-brown.

I let the plug out. A sucking sound erupted from the whirlpool going down the drain. The puppy climbed up the side of the bath to get away from the monster. I pushed water into the drain, getting rid of the vortex. Clare couldn't hold him. I caught him before he launched off the side. Now I was as wet as Clare.

"This is a disaster," I said.

She sat on the ground and laughed. I sat and held the puppy to my chest and laughed with her.

"We still have to rinse him," she said between breaths. I glanced between the puppy and the bath. It had to be done. Then I peered at Clare.

She'd never looked so beautiful. Dirt was smudged across her face. Her hair was wet in patches. The wet t-shirt clung to her, showing me exactly how the girl I loved had turned into a woman.

Shit, she was hot.

CHAPTER SIXTEEN

Clare

Beau licked his lips. He leaned in closer to me. A few more inches and we'd be touching. My lips ached for his. Goosebumps erupted on my skin. My breathing shallowed as he got closer. Closer still. I took in his face, his eyes, his lips. Those soft lips.

He jerked back. The puppy's head came between us. He squirmed, reached out and licked my face. My stomach dropped. As adorable as he was, he was not the male I wanted kissing me.

The spell was broken. Beau turned back to the bath. "I'll hold him. You rinse."

I nodded. When the puppy was all clean, I wrapped him in a fluffy towel and rubbed him dry. Beau stood up. His t-shirt was so wet it would start dripping at any moment.

"You're soaked. I'll get you something to wear."

I placed the puppy on the ground and left the room. I blushed as I thought about the near kiss and how much I wanted it. What was I thinking? I wasn't thinking, that was the problem. I grabbed a t-shirt out of my drawer and smiled to myself. I couldn't wait to see him put it on.

When I got back, Beau had taken his t-shirt off and was patting his skin dry. I stopped in the doorway. Beau Hart was a fine specimen of a man. That body was not one I recognised or one I'd ever forget. Toned stomach. Toned chest. He wasn't all muscle, but everything was clearly defined. Someone who worked out but still liked food. Such a stupid saying, but fitting.

There was a tattoo over his heart. I stepped closer to see it. Two honeycomb pieces beside each other with a bee inside each, so delicate and perfect in design, I could see the tiny, fragile hairs and imagined the bags of pollen they'd collect on their legs. I moved closer, my hand reaching out to touch the ink. There were initials inside each honeycomb —CW and BH. Holy shit, he had our initials tattooed over his heart.

I shoved the t-shirt in his direction, not even looking at him, and bent to pick up the towels. He had our initials tattooed over his heart, on that perfect body. Maybe it wasn't perfect, I don't know, it had been a long time since I'd seen a naked torso, his naked torso.

"Do you think this will fit?" Beau asked, holding the pink t-shirt out in front of him.

"It's stretchy."

"You couldn't have chosen another colour? I'm sure you've got a million black ones."

"I think pink will complement your skin."

He looked at the slogan, *Girl Power*, and gave me a crooked smile.

"I wanted to remind you of the balance of power."

"I'm fully aware of who holds the power in this relationship." He pulled the t-shirt over his head. It stretched but was tight in places. It revealed his midriff and muscles and didn't leave enough to my imagination. That idea had backfired on me. At this point in time, I had no damn power at all and definitely no fucking willpower.

"I'm going to take the puppy to the laundry to give him his flea treatment. Most of the fleas would have come out with the bath. He and Clementine will need to stay separated for a few hours just in case." I pointed to the right. "The lounge room is that way."

BEAU'S low voice was coming from the lounge room. He was talking to Clementine. I listened from the bedroom.

"Thank you for looking after Clare."

I pulled my wet t-shirt over my head.

"I know, you're right; she didn't need much looking after."

Oh, but I did.

I rummaged in the drawer for one of my million black t-shirts.

"I missed you. I made sure I said hello to every black cat I ever met."

My heart melted. Why was I eavesdropping? I mean, it was just a man talking to a cat. But it was revealing. I tugged the t-shirt over my head. Beau laughed. A soft sound.

"None of them drooled like you, though."

I walked to the door.

"I think your owner nearly drooled before."

Shithead.

I made my footsteps loud as I approached the lounge.

The bloody traitor of a cat was lying in Beau's arms, smooching him.

"In your dreams," I said, drawing his attention to me.

"What?"

"I was not drooling over you."

Beau and Clementine gazed at each other. Beau chuckled. Clementine purred so loudly I could hear her from where I was standing.

"Clementine disagrees."

"She wasn't there."

Beau indicated to his wet arm. Clementine sure was in good form. "Like cat, like owner."

"We need to take photos of the puppy," I said. There was no way I was admitting anything to Beau about drooling, kissing or any of the other things I might fantasise about tonight.

"Trying to get rid of him already?"

"Trying to get rid of you more like it."

Beau stood up and placed Clementine on the couch. She stretched and rolled onto her back. Beau patted her exposed tummy. She stretched a bit further.

I would have words with her later.

She couldn't fall for him again.

It was too dangerous.

CHAPTER SEVENTEEN

Beau

"What are you wearing?" Mike asked.

I groaned. I hadn't had time to get changed. "Nothing."

"Show me."

"Give me a minute to get changed."

"Not before you show me your t-shirt."

There was no point denying him. I held the phone out so he could see it. Bastard took a photo.

"Are you finished?" I asked.

"As soon as I send it to Lisa, I am."

I ignored that and relayed the day to him.

"What are you going to do if no one claims the puppy?"

"Keep it, I guess."

"You're going to keep the puppy?" He raised his eyebrows.

"He's awfully cute."

Mike sighed. "You can't keep a puppy based on its cuteness."

"The puppy needs a home. I need a home. We can have one together."

"What's wrong with your parent's place?"

"There's nothing wrong with it, but I think having my own place would be good."

"So, your own place and a puppy. That's a big commitment," Mike said. He was watching me closely.

"I think I'm ready. I don't want to be anywhere else."

"And this has nothing to do with Clare?"

"No." I shrugged. There was no point lying to him. "Not entirely." Mostly.

"And you didn't move back for Clare?"

"Not entirely." Mostly.

"Let's go back a bit. You've told me how close you were growing up. You've told me about your one and only kiss. Did you always want to be more than just friends?"

I rested my hand on my leg. Mike wouldn't need to see the pressure as I pressed; the movement of my shoulder would have told him.

"We were always more than friends."

"In what way?"

"Clare Walker was my entire world. Some days when I didn't want to get up, she was the sole reason I did."

"Do you think she felt the same way? You've never clarified that for me."

"I don't know. I never told her how I felt."

"Why not?"

He knew the answer to this. It was always the same answer.

"I didn't feel worthy. And I didn't want to ruin our friendship."

"Do you feel worthy now?"

"Maybe."

"Beau, you will never feel worthy until you talk to her, until you stop carrying around this guilt you have."

I looked down at my feet. "I know."

"Do you have a photo of this puppy?"

I sent him a photo.

"He is cute. I can see how he brought the two of you together."

I laughed at him. "I can't just rely on cute, though."

"No, if you could rely on cute, you'd have had your lady on day one."

"Ha ha."

"The next time we talk, I want you to have spoken to Clare about the kiss and your feelings."

Ha! He was pulling out the mentor card. I nodded. How on Earth was I going to do that? Opening my heart to her was dangerous. It could get broken in two seconds flat.

"I know it's scary putting your heart out there, but you can't move forward until you've dealt with the past."

"I know."

I hung up. That damn kiss. The damn perfect kiss. It was time it stopped haunting me and became something we could build upon instead.

CLARE WAS WAITING under the tree. I turned my car off and sat for a second. This would be the last time I'd see her. My last chance to tell her how much she meant to me. The words ran around in my head. Thank you. Thank you for the last seventeen years that you kept me sane. You supported me even when you didn't know you supported me. Thank you. I'm going to miss you.

I got out of the car and walked to her. Bees buzzed out of their hives, intent on finding their morning fix. They didn't come near us, but I could nearly feel their buzzing in my veins.

Clare met me halfway. Her hand went to my hair and pushed it out of my face. All the words I'd been practising for days, weeks even, disappeared.

"Well, this is it," she said.

"Yep."

"I hope you find what you're looking for out there."

The world was full of possibilities. But the possibility of Clare sharing it with me was non-existent—she needed to stay with her family. I moved in closer to her, studying her features. I didn't need to store them in my memory. They'd been scorched there. Thousands of tiny memories combined. I needed to tell her everything I felt for her. But what was the point? I was the one leaving her.

I took her hands and marvelled at how they fit in mine. Slow, almost painful energy stretched from our hands to my stomach. It knotted.

I needed to tell her. Tell her what?

I moved closer to her. Her brown eyes, the only eyes that ever truly saw me, searched my face.

I didn't need words. Words would never be enough. Then I did something I'd been dreaming of for months. I let go of my seventeen-year-old best friend's hands, and I kissed her. And kissed her. Her lips responded. My breath hitched. I took in every moment, natural and needy, and placed it with all my other memories of Clare. The way her lips moved with mine. The wetness of her mouth. Then as she pressed against me, I stopped recording every moment and simply lived it.

The knot in my stomach unfurled, and warmth spread through me like the unfurling of apple blossoms in spring. Everywhere we touched, the cells of my skin felt like they were melting into others. Aching need followed.

My lips slowed. My breath was ragged. She was everything I'd ever need, everything I'd ever want. I rested my forehead on hers, not daring to open my eyes. When my legs steadied enough for me to finally step away, my eyes opened to hers.

I could only manage four words. "I love you, Clare."

Before she said a word, I turned and walked to my car, leaving behind the only person I could ever love.

CHAPTER EIGHTEEN

Clare

I PULLED INTO MY DRIVEWAY. Beau's car was in the carport. I glanced around at my yard. The lawn was freshly mown, even the edges were done. I left those half the time. It was bad enough having to mow, let alone use the whipper snipper.

As soon as I opened the car door, I could hear his cheerful voice from the backyard. I opened the gate and watched as he ran around with Dozer chasing him. The puppy was growing bigger every day. I swear he had doubled in size in two weeks.

Beau stopped running and smiled over at me. My stomach squeezed. Why the hell did it keep doing that? Here, Beau was so carefree, unlike at work, where he was more serious. Dozer ran over to me, his tongue lolling. He sat at my feet, his golden-brown eyes gazing up at me, expectant. I crouched down to pat him.

"Thanks for mowing," I said.

"No problem. I'm happy to help."

Beau was always happy to help. At work, he'd put up his hand if something needed to be done. At first, I thought it was because he was trying to make himself look good. And I wanted to believe that. I didn't want to believe in a good Beau. But when I thought about it, Beau had always been like that. When Mum had been sick, and we all knew she wasn't going to get better, I insisted she come home so one of us would be with her when she died. Beau had been with me every day, helping in any way he could. Sometimes he sat with Mum and read to her to help her get through the day. No, Beau didn't help to make himself look better. Beau helped because he was a good person.

Did everyone at work see that? I was a hard but fair manager. Beau's approach was different. Maybe people preferred that. Maybe his dad saw the benefits in the way Beau went about his work. I always put in extra hours because I thought that's what was wanted from me. I wanted to get things done when I thought they needed to be done. So did Beau, but he approached it in a different way. He was more collaborative. Did I have to be more like Beau to get Justin's attention?

Dozer flopped at Beau's feet.

"You may have actually tired him out," I said.

"Let's see. He might find some extra energy when he gets inside and sees Clementine."

That was true. I went to the back door, expecting Beau to follow. I turned to see him still standing where I'd left him. He was looking down at his feet. When he raised his eyes to mine, he said, "I have ingredients for California Waffles in the car. Would you like me to make them for dinner?"

Not just dinner but him cooking me dinner. This was crossing into new territory. We had pizza last night and beers on the deck the night before. And it was all too easy. Every night when he left, I reminded myself what was at risk.

"California Waffles?" I couldn't help myself. No wasn't in me.

"Waffles, southern fried chicken, maple syrup, bacon and ice cream."

"So, like a main and dessert in one?"

"Precisely."

"OK. Waffles it is."

I wasn't going to say no, but he probably already knew that. It would be rude to say no. And I would have nothing for dinner.

I waited for Beau by the back door. Dozer followed him to the gate and all the way back, his tail wagging the whole time. I opened the door, and he trotted inside. So much for using all of his energy. By the time we made it down the hallway, he was playing with Clementine, jumping from side to side while she stared at him. As soon as I approached, she gave me a withering look.

"The babysitter isn't impressed." Beau chuckled beside me.

He turned towards the kitchen, but I grabbed his arm to stop him. "Wait."

Clementine stayed still until Dozer stopped bouncing, then made her move. She ran up the hall with Dozer chasing, turned around at the end and leapt over him on her return journey. Dozer didn't have the same agility and ran for a few more steps before turning around. Clementine sat, waiting for him to catch up before taking off again.

"She has it all figured out," Beau said.

"And as soon as she says stop, he does."

"She tells him to stop?"

"She'll sit still and start licking her paw. If he keeps trying to play, she'll turn her back on him."

Beau laughed. The rich sound warmed my insides.

I rolled my eyes at myself and turned towards him. "What can I do to help with dinner?"

"We'll start with the chicken."

He began unpacking the bag of ingredients, placing them onto the bench. His hand hesitated in the bag. He pulled out something red and handed it to me—a Cherry Ripe Easter Egg. "This is for you."

It was my favourite Easter egg—rich dark chocolate with Cherry Ripe pieces embedded in it. I glanced at the egg and then his face. His Adam's apple bobbed. The tips of his ears turned red. Reaching out, I took the egg from him, slow, gentle, as if it would break.

"Thank you." My voice was quiet, shaky.

"It's still your favourite, isn't it?"

I nodded, not trusting my voice. I turned it in my hands as if I was staring at the crown jewels.

"You can't eat it now. It's for Sunday." The smile in his voice had me looking back at him. He smirked.

"You know there is no such rule."

"Yeah, OK. Maybe save it for dessert." He laughed, and my insides swirled like melted chocolate.

I placed the egg down as Beau continued to get the ingredients out. He started to give directions.

"You learnt to cook this in California?" I asked as I followed his first instruction.

"Yes, but they didn't originate there. No one could actually tell me where they came from or why they're called California Waffles. We sort of guessed it was from the south, seeing it has southern fried chicken."

"It sure is an eclectic mix of ingredients. The bacon and maple syrup make me think of Canada."

We worked side by side, Beau giving instructions and me following them.

"What else did you learn to cook in California?"

"There were some Mexicans on staff who cooked burritos. The flavour in the meat was amazing." He looked over at me as I coated the chicken. My fingers were covered in egg and coating. "You know the coating is supposed to go on the chicken?"

I laughed. "I'm trying."

He gave me a hip bump and a smile. "Keep trying."

He watched me as I coated the next piece. Without glancing at him, I couldn't tell if he was studying my technique or me. I suspected the latter. Goosebumps erupted on my skin. I concentrated harder on the chicken.

When he started cooking, I leant against the counter, admiring him from behind. It would have been so much easier if he didn't look so good, if his arse wasn't so well proportioned.

This was insane. Being attracted to Beau was insane. Spending time with Beau was insane. And feeling like we were friends was beyond insane.

I SAT IN OUR OFFICE, answering emails. Beau had gone to speak to the foremen about rosters. Thoughts of him crept into my head. The way he laughed with abandon at Dozer and Clementine reminded me of when we were children and spent many hours alone together. Being alone together was a habit we were falling back into, at work and at home.

What scared me was that being alone with him wasn't bad. In fact, it was nice. Like his body was nice. And that tattoo was nice. My stomach flipped. It was intimidating knowing someone had your initials tattooed on their body.

I had a million questions. I had no right to ask them. I shouldn't want to ask them. I wouldn't. But they were at the forefront of my mind anyway. Why did he get it? When did he get it? Did it hurt? Did he draw it himself? It was something he would do. I had a whole sketchpad of his drawings at home. He gave it to me before he left because he knew I loved them.

Beau walked into the office, pulling me out of my thoughts. "Charli said she received another big order today from a mainland nursery."

Charli? "I thought you were speaking to the foremen."

"I was. I took her some apples on the way back."

I'm sure she could have gotten her own. She didn't need to be waited on. By him.

"She showed me the email. Have a look at it."

He came and stood beside me. Right beside me. Tingles ran through me.

Had they been this close to each other while she *showed* him the email?

I swapped over to the nursery inbox. Beau rested his hand on my shoulder as he leant forward to point at the email. Heat spread from his hand to my whole body as if his hand was an incubator.

I willed my hand to move the mouse to the email. I opened it and started reading. Beau's hand remained. It took a lot of effort to concentrate on the words and not on the feel of his strong hand.

. . .

HI CHARLI,

Thank you for your delivery of our first order. The trees you supplied were top quality. We've told other local nurseries about your trees and impeccable service. We would like to place another order for forty trees and discuss the possibility of a standing order going forward.

Regards

Jeremy

"ISN'T IT GREAT?" he asked. "That's all your hard work paying off."

I looked up and met his eyes. He smiled down at me. A jolt ran through me, starting from my heart. I could be lost in those intense green eyes forever.

"Thank you."

His hand left my shoulder. I wanted it back.

What? No, I didn't. His touch was as unnerving as his display of pride.

CHAPTER NINETEEN

Beau

I STOOD beside Nan in the kitchen, chopping vegetables for the salad.

"How do you want me to chop the cucumber?" Nan asked.

"Dice it, please."

"Would you often have salads with your meals in Italy?"

"Yes. It adds freshness to the meal. Sometimes, we'd finish with fresh fruit too."

Nan chopped the cucumber with skill, and I pushed the Roma tomatoes towards her. "Like this?" she asked, holding the knife long ways.

"Yes."

"What sort of fresh fruit?"

"Peaches, nectarines, prickly pears."

"Prickly pears, wouldn't they be hard to peel?"

"There's a trick to that. You soak them first to make the skin soft."

"That's smart," Pop said from the dining table. "They're a pest in Australia. Never thought of eating them. Do they taste nice?"

"Yes. It's hard to explain the taste. They're sweet."

"How's work?" Nan asked as she turned the oven light on to check the lasagne.

"I don't feel as lost anymore." Being here with Nan and Pop was easier than being at home with my parents. I didn't have to worry about what I said or what they were thinking.

Pop looked up from the crossword he was doing. "You mean Clare is actually letting you do stuff?"

I laughed. He knew his granddaughter well. "Yes."

"It would be good for her to share the load," Nan said. "Maybe she'll stop working long hours."

I nodded. "She's always there before me. And after. But this week, she's been getting home earlier."

Pop tilted his head. "How do you know?"

"I go there every day to play with Dozer or take him for a walk."

That wasn't the only reason I went there. But it was the only reason I'd admit to out loud.

"Right," Pop said, his lips lifting on one side. I wasn't fooling him.

"So, things are better with Clare?" Nan asked as I handed the bowl of salad to her to dress.

There were many ways I could answer that. "I don't think she wants to stab me on a daily basis anymore."

Pop laughed. "Well, that's a start."

Some days I thought we were getting on great, finding our way back to our friendship. She'd smile or laugh, and it was like the path to the future was lit for me. Each smile or peal of laughter brought me closer to where I wanted to be.

Other days she gave me the cold shoulder or avoided me. She wasn't rude, just withdrawn. And the path that had been lit now led into a dark forest.

I wanted to talk to her, to tell her how I felt being back home. All of it. I wanted us to share our thoughts like we did when we were younger. Eight years had changed us both. Not only were our bodies separated, but our hearts were too. I hoped it wouldn't take eight years to bring us back together again. Another eight years would mean nearly half our lives without each other.

The back door opened, and I turned to see Clare. I braced myself for her reaction. The first time she'd found me here, she hadn't been impressed. It was the same the second, third and fourth times. But after that, her teeth clenched less, her hard stare softened and she opened up a little more.

She rolled her eyes at me. "I should have known you'd be here. Like I don't see enough of you at work."

Her voice was light. My muscles released.

"I hear you've been seeing Beau more than just at work," Pop said. I swear he liked to stir the honey pot.

"He comes to visit Dozer," Clare said.

"I'm sure he does."

Ignoring him, Clare walked to the freezer. "I've brought salted honey ice cream for dessert."

"Did you make it?" I asked.

"I can cook, you know," Clare said as she peered inside the oven.

"Making ice cream hardly constitutes cooking," Pop said.

"I can do more than just make ice cream."

"You should cook for Beau," Pop suggested.

"Why would I do that?" Clare said as she got cutlery out to set the table.

"You know, the way to a man's heart and all," Pop said.

Clare stopped in her tracks and stared at me. "Is that why you've been cooking for me?"

"I didn't know you were a man," I replied.

Nan took the lasagne out of the oven, a small smile on her face.

GOING to the gym was my quiet time. The time when I emptied my mind and instead of thinking about a million things, I only concentrated on the weights I was lifting. But this morning, I couldn't stop thinking about Clare. Last night at Nan and Pop's, I'd still held back. I had the perfect opportunity to share my feelings but hadn't.

If I wanted a future with Clare, I needed to open up. We both did. That defining moment when I'd left needed to be spoken about. But what if it tore us apart forever?

I increased the weight on the bar and started my squats. I watched myself in the mirror, forcing myself to concentrate on my form and counting my reps. By the time I counted to ten, my legs were struggling. I set the bar down and had a drink of water.

Last night wasn't a waste, though. Clare sat close to me, like when we were younger. We'd all enjoyed each other's company, speaking about all kinds of things. Nan enjoyed hearing about the festivals and religious feasts in Italy. She'd had an Italian friend in school who lived in a nursing home now. I'd decided I'd try to make time to visit her. We could have a good old chin wag in Italian.

Talk, that's what Clare and I needed to do. I didn't need to declare my love for Clare. This wasn't a go-big-or-go-home situation. What I needed to do was be vulnerable. I needed to trust her enough to show her a little part of me. Not a part I showed the whole world, a part just for her.

CHAPTER TWENTY

Clare

Beau was already in when I walked into our office. Our office. *Ours*. A word I didn't think I would say in a hundred years. Beau was on his phone, tapping and swiping.

"Still no news on the puppy," he said.

I nodded. I suspected that would be the case. I'd searched the local pages and hadn't found any posts about lost puppies that fit the description. And it had already been two weeks with no response to our posts.

"Would you be able to keep him for a few more days, please? I need to find a rental that will take pets."

"You're going to keep him?"

"I'd like to."

I sat down at my desk and turned the computer on. My stomach was tossing and turning like me on a sleepless night. If Beau was going to find a rental and keep the puppy, did that mean he was going to stay? Maybe not; a rental didn't have to be forever. A puppy was for life, but he could take a dog with him anywhere.

"Clare?"

"Huh?"

"Would you mind keeping him for a few more days?"

"No, that's fine. He and Clementine are inseparable."

"Thank you."

That would mean more visits from Beau. He'd been around every day since we'd found the puppy. He'd bought dinner for us one night and had cooked on others. It was all happening too fast. Us falling back into our easy friendship. What about the orchard? If he stayed, would there be room enough for both of us?

I opened my emails. There was one from Justin. He'd put a deadline on our ideas. He wanted us to present them to him after the Apple and Fruit Growers Conference and Dinner in June. That was two months away.

"Did you see the email from your dad?"

"Yeah. Do you want me to start putting the ideas and all our research into a presentation?"

Did I want him to do that? I'd rather do it myself and delve a little deeper. But surely, I could trust him. Besides, I'd review it all before we presented it.

"That would be great, thanks."

We worked in silence for a while. It wasn't like the first few weeks he was here where I couldn't stand being near him longer than I had to. It was comfortable now. Mostly. I still had a lot of questions for him that we both seemed to be avoiding.

"Clare?"

"Yeah?" I continued to scan the figures in front of me.

"You know your dad's housewarming party?" His voice was higher than usual.

"Yeah."

"I'm nervous about going on my own. I might not know

many people, and I haven't been to many social events since I got back."

"OK."

Was he trying to ask something? Of course he was. I was such an idiot. I needed to remember this new Beau was still the old Beau. "Why don't you come with us? I was going to pick Nan and Pop up around six."

"Thank you. I mean I could go with Mum and Dad, but I don't know...Shall I pick you up, and then we can get Nan and Pop?"

"Yes." I closed the spreadsheet I had open. "Beau, you don't need to hide your feelings from me. If you're nervous or anxious, tell me. Don't dwell on it." I paused; this was not safe. We couldn't be who we used to be. My heart couldn't bear being broken again. But I couldn't stop myself. "I'm here for you."

Silence from the other side. No keys or mouse clicking. Beau rolled his chair to the side.

"Thank you. I try to talk myself through things. It usually works. I can usually sort through what's real and what's anxiety. But sometimes I can't." He looked down at the desk. I imagined him processing his words. He looked up and gave me a brave smile. "Thank you."

"No worries. What are friends for?"

Is that what we were? Friends? I don't remember ever having checked out my other friends' bodies or wanting to kiss them.

I HEARD Beau's car pull up in the driveway, then his door open and close. I wiped my hands on my jeans. I'd checked myself at least ten times in the last fifteen minutes. My high-waisted jeans and flowy crop top looked fine. What was I so worried about? It wasn't like I was going on a date.

I opened the door. Beau stood there in jeans and a button-down shirt. Jeez, he looked good. Good enough to...

"You look nice," he said. He leant in and kissed my cheek.

I blushed. "Thanks. So do you."

"How's Dozer?"

I blocked the doorway. "Sleeping. Don't disturb him."

His face dropped. I ushered him back onto the deck.

"We don't have time anyway. Nan and Pop are waiting for us."

He nodded. We walked to the car together. He opened the door for me and closed it after I hopped in. This was not a date.

"I like your new hair colour," Beau said when he got into the car. He'd said that each time I'd changed it.

I kept my hands tucked firmly between my legs where they were safe.

"Thanks. I thought apple green would be nice for Dad. Green is his favourite colour."

"Always an apple colour?"

"Yeah, that's what we do—live and breathe apples."

That's all my life had been for the last seven years. Beau turned onto the main road and headed to the orchard.

"No chance of you dying it my favourite colour, then."

"Never seen a blue apple."

"Well, there are Blue Pearmain apples."

"They're not really blue, though."

"Black Diamond apple?"

"You're making this shit up."

"Google it."

I did. They were indeed real apples. "Not blue."

"Keep googling. Surely there's a blue one somewhere."

I did as he asked, but there were no blue apples to be found.

"Sorry, no blue apples."

"Lucked out again."

He pulled up into Nan and Pop's driveway and got out of the car. I watched as Nan came out and kissed his cheek. Pop followed and shook his hand. Anyone would think they didn't see each other practically every other day. Beau took Nan to the rear passenger-side door and made sure she got in OK before getting back in.

"It's been a while since we've been on a double date, hasn't it, Pop?"

"Way too long." He leant over and gave her a kiss.

Beau gave me a grin. I let her cheeky comment slide. She was only baiting me.

"When Pop and I went on dates, he would always hold my hand while driving."

I shoved my hands firmer into my lap. This was not a date.

"Don't lie. Pop would've been too busy holding onto the steering wheel because you didn't have power steering," I said.

I laughed as Pop screwed up his mouth.

"But we did end all of our dates with a goodnight kiss," Nan said.

"It was the best part," Pop added.

"We'll need to keep a close eye on the two of you." Nan's voice was full of humour.

"Shame. Beau will be dropping you off first," I said.

This was not a date.

CHAPTER TWENTY-ONE

Beau

WE PULLED up outside Glen and Gloria's new house. It was an old house that had been modernised by rendering out the front and a fresh colour scheme. The driveway was steep, and I imagined the views from the house were spectacular.

I went around the other side of the car. Clare had opened her door by the time I got there. I helped Nan out and started walking up the driveway with her. She was still young and fit for her seventy years, but I didn't want any accidents on my watch.

"It's OK, you can just take my wife," Pop called out.

Nan patted my arm. "Thank you, Beau."

Pop chatted to Clare as they followed. "How's your date with Beau going?"

"It's not a date." Her words were clear and forceful.

"So, no goodnight kiss tonight. That's a shame."

"You and Nan can make up for it."

I knocked on the door. A lady opened it. Her brown

hair was tied back in a ponytail, and her cheeks were flushed. She took hold of my hand. "You must be Beau. It's so nice to meet you. I'm Gloria, Glen's partner."

"Nice to meet you too."

I stepped past her and stood in the foyer while she greeted Nan, Pop and Clare.

She took me by the arm and led us down the hallway.

"How did you enjoy living in Europe, Beau? I spent a summer there many years ago."

"I loved it. It was amazing how you could travel through so many countries in a day."

"Did you get much chance to travel when you were working?"

"There wasn't much to spend money on during the season, seeing we worked such long hours. So when I was able to get leave, I had money saved."

"I loved Paris. So rich in culture," she said. She turned me to a beautiful painting of the Eiffel Tower at dusk. "I bought this in one of the street markets."

"Parisians love those markets," I said as we moved on.

She ushered us down the hallway, which opened into an open-plan living area and expansive deck. When she let go of me, she hung back to speak to Clare. "Oh, Clare, he's adorable."

Clare didn't respond.

Glen approached us next. He looked the same as when I'd left—tall with closely cropped, greying brown hair. Back then, he was withered like an apple that had fallen from a tree. I wondered if he'd ever feel happy again. Now he was rehydrated, fresh. Must have been his new life with Gloria. Second love was good for him. I'd never been able to get over my first one.

"Beau, it's great to see you again." He clapped my shoulder. "Come out onto the deck."

Clare stuck close to me but didn't interact. Her mood had changed. She stood there, her arms crossed, her jaw set. What happened? It all seemed to stem from the date comments. It didn't need to be a date. I mean, I wanted it to be. But if she wasn't comfortable with the idea, what could I do to reassure her it was OK?

"Would you like a drink?" I asked her.

"No thanks." Her voice was sarcastic.

I stood next to her, looking down at my feet. "Sorry if I'm making you feel uncomfortable."

"I'm not uncomfortable." She unfolded and refolded her arms.

Gloria approached. "Clare, Beau, could you please get some wine from the cellar? Two whites and two reds."

Clare nodded.

"It's just down the stairs."

Clare trudged down the stairs. There was nothing to do but follow. She went from one wine rack to another, not choosing but staring and huffing before changing direction.

I needed to ask her what was wrong. It wasn't going to go well, given the mood she was in. But if I didn't ask her, we would never get anything out into the open. We'd always have this festering sore bothering us.

"What's wrong?"

I stood in the middle of the room and let her prowl the edges.

"Why would anything be wrong?" She swung to the next wall.

"I don't know. That's why I'm asking."

She turned on me faster than a swarm of bees. "I don't

know, Beau. Everyone out there thinks we're on a date or we're a couple or something fucking ridiculous."

Would that be so bad? I didn't dare ask the question.

"Why would I want to date someone who treated me like shit? I mean, why the fuck did you even kiss me? Was it some sort of stupid power play?"

"That's—"

"And then you turned around and fucking left." Her eyes were wide as she stared at me, daring me to speak. "What sort of person does that?" She didn't wait for me to answer. "Not even just left but cut off all fucking contact."

Her fists were clenched by her side, and her face was red.

"When my life was falling apart around me—practically getting kicked out of school, Tahlia being a psychotic teenager, my dad withdrawing—when I needed you, you didn't answer my call."

"I'm sorry."

"You're sorry?" she shouted.

"Yes, I shouldn't have kissed you."

"Then why did you? We were never a couple. We were friends. For seventeen years of my life, we were just friends, and then the day you were leaving, you decided, what, that you'd just see what it felt like?"

For eight years, that kiss had haunted my memories, every cell reliving the feeling, my heart breaking all over again.

"No, I didn't just *decide*. You were more than just my friend. You were my life. I loved you more than life itself."

I started pacing. I needed her to understand. She'd never understand. I pressed my hands against my legs. I'd fucked it up so bad.

"You loved me? When I needed you the most, I reached

out to you, even though I hadn't heard from you in six months. And all you did was fucking ignore pathetic little me."

I stopped pacing. "I couldn't—"

"You couldn't what?"

"I couldn't—" I clutched at my leg.

"What? What couldn't you do?"

"I couldn't speak to you because I was going to take my own life. I couldn't let you be the last person to speak to me. I couldn't let you feel the guilt and pain. I. Just. Couldn't."

"You what?"

I sank down to the ground, leaning against a post. "My anxiety had hit an all-time high. It wouldn't shut up with the questions and accusations. You say you were pathetic? I was the one who was pathetic. Six months away from home, from you, and that's where I ended up. So much for making it on my own."

Tears rolled down my cheeks.

"Beau—"

"Don't you see, Clare? I was never worthy of you. That kiss was me being weak. I wanted to feel what it was like, just once. I had all these words to say to you, but they wouldn't come."

Clare's shoulders dropped, and her face softened. "Why didn't you tell me?"

"I don't want your pity. All I ever wanted was to be enough for you."

"You were enough."

"Bull."

"Do you think I'd have ever done half the things we did if you weren't by my side?"

"What?"

"I wouldn't have been brave enough without you by my side. It was your support and belief in me."

That wasn't right. It was the other way around. I shook my head and stood up. "Don't say that just because you feel sorry for me." I wasn't going to be pitied, especially by her.

"What?"

"You heard me."

She walked up to me. She was so close I could see her shaking.

"You think I feel sorry for you? I have many more feelings than just sorry."

She turned around, walked two steps and turned back.

"Beau Hart, I've never been so angry in my life." She pointed her finger at me. "I want to punch you, no, knee you in the balls and then as you crumple to your knees, I'll uppercut you under the chin."

I closed my stance but stood my ground. Why did she always have to be so descriptive? Better than a pruning saw, I guess. Imagine what she'd do with that.

"Then maybe you'll see that you were always enough for me."

I covered the distance between us and pulled her towards me. She was still angry. I knew she could maim me right then and there. But I wanted to kiss her, to taste her.

I didn't hesitate.

CHAPTER TWENTY-TWO

Clare

I KISSED Beau like he was the first man I'd ever kissed and would be the last.

I pressed my body against him as our lips parted. He tasted like fresh mint, delicate and sweet. Clutching at the back of his shirt, I pulled it taut. Searing heat spread through me, and the coolness of the air surrounding us disappeared. We could have been in the storeroom at work, and the air still would have sizzled.

Beau's lips slowed. My heartbeat didn't. Neither did my breathing. This one kiss, it wasn't enough. He could kiss me when I was angry, happy or any emotion in between, and it would never be enough. He pulled away, but I still held onto him. His soft lips brushed mine once, twice. Serenity entered every cell like a bee being smoked and spreading pheromones.

We stepped apart, the space between us growing. A small smile played on Beau's lips. "Does this mean we're on a date?"

"I'll think about it."

"Maybe a second kiss will convince you." He reached for me.

The door to the cellar opened.

"Are you two bringing up some wine or what?" Tahlia called down the stairs.

My stomach dropped.

"Coming," I answered. I turned to Beau. "Missed your chance."

"There'll be plenty more."

We grabbed some bottles and went upstairs. I let him go first so I could enjoy the view. As soon as we got through the door, Tahlia threw herself at Beau, hugging him and then pulling him away. If she wasn't my sister, I might have been jealous. I carried the wine to the table on the deck.

Dad was talking to his friends. I went over to join them. He put an arm around my shoulders and kissed the top of my head.

"Gloria knew straight away that this was the one. I think the deck and view won her over."

Tahlia and Beau were still speaking.

"It's fantastic," I said, joining the conversation. "We can enjoy some good meals out here in summer."

"And the fireplace will be great in winter."

Tahlia was showing Beau something on her phone. He nodded with enthusiasm and pointed at something. I listened as Dad spoke but didn't pay much attention.

"I'm going to help Gloria," I said, stepping away.

She was at the island preparing platters with King Island cheese, kabana, olives, dips and crackers. I glanced at Beau and Tahlia. Beau was watching me. My stomach flipped. I turned my attention back to the task at hand.

"Do you want me to take these out?"

"Yes, please."

I took a platter out to the deck and was returning to collect another when Tahlia took my hand.

"What's with you and Beau?"

"Nothing is with Beau and me," I said as we walked into the kitchen. I was going to grab another platter, but Tahlia seized both my hands.

"Don't lie. Every time I look, one of you is watching the other." Shrewd as ever.

Gloria looked between us and grabbed a platter. "I'll take the rest out."

"Well?" Tahlia prodded.

"We kissed."

"You and Beau kissed?" Her voice was high. "Like kissed kissed?"

"What other kissing is there?"

"Don't be difficult."

"Fine. OK, we kissed kissed."

Her hands squeezed mine. "And?"

"It was nice."

"Nice? You haven't seen each other for eight years, and it was just *nice*? That must be disappointing."

I huffed. Jeez, she was pushy. "It was in no way disappointing."

"Huh," she said with triumph in her voice.

Gloria came back and left again. Great help I was.

"Does that mean you're finally getting together?"

I glanced at Beau, who was standing with his parents.

"I don't know."

"Why don't you know?"

"We hadn't spoken in eight years. That's a long time. And what about work?"

"Are you seriously thinking about work?"

I shrugged.

"The way I see it, Justin is making you work together for a reason...because he wants you to work together."

"I suppose."

"You know what I think?"

There was no point answering. She was going to tell me anyway. She rubbed my arm.

"You're scared. It's OK to be scared, natural even. But you need to stop making excuses. You two are perfect for each other."

I *was* scared. Heartbreak does that to a person.

"You'd be stupid to waste any more time."

I nodded. Time to take a chance.

Tahlia dragged me outside and left me standing beside Beau.

"Did that smart sister of yours give you a pep talk too?"

I laughed. "Yes."

Beau reached out and took my hand. I held on tight.

"SO, YOU AND BEAU?" Pop asked.

He cracked the beehive open with the hive tool. It was a decent crack. The bees had done a good job sealing the hive.

"Beau and I what?"

"Heard you had a kiss."

"Did you just?" Surely Beau hadn't been here already to talk to Pop.

"That's what Tahlia said."

"Big mouth."

Pop pulled a frame out and examined it. I got closer. The bee suit swished as I walked. He turned the frame for me to see. Only one side was filled with honey. He put it back in. He grabbed another frame and lugged it out. "This one is heavier."

He turned it for me to see. It was capped on both sides. I handed him a soft brush so he could remove the bees without hurting them. He placed the frame in a wheelbarrow, and I covered it with a soft blanket. If we didn't hide it, the bees would come for it.

"So, is *everything* out in the open now?" Pop asked.

"Mostly."

"What do you mean mostly?"

"I didn't bring up work."

"Why not? If you're worried about it, you should tell him."

I shrugged. Pop pulled another frame out. "What did you speak about then?"

"How he left. How he never made contact."

Pop put a third frame in the wheelbarrow.

"And what did he say?"

Pop put the lid back on the hive and pushed the wheelbarrow to the porch. His silence told me he knew. He knew that Beau had wanted to end his life.

"Why didn't you tell me?" I asked.

"It wasn't for me to share."

He was right, just like it wasn't for me to share. I doubted his parents knew. They couldn't accept that there had been something wrong when he was growing up. Maybe they didn't understand, but there was more in mainstream media today about mental illness. And given that Beau's great-grandfather had PTSD after the war, it should have been easier for them to acknowledge.

"So, he's staying then?"

I nodded. "He's looking for a place to rent so he can keep Dozer."

"Good."

Pop pulled a frame out and rested it on the extractor. He used the uncapping fork to scrape off the top layer of wax. The fork caused minimal damage to the honeycomb beneath, so it was easier for the bees to rebuild the frame.

"You know, when I first started keeping bees, it was in the summertime. The bees were always on the go, collecting and making honey. When winter came, it made sense. They were nowhere to be seen. All that honey they'd been making sustained them."

Pop put the frame in the extractor and got another frame out to prepare.

"For a long time, you reminded me of the bees."

I watched Pop as he scraped the frame. His strong hands were gentle in their action. "You were always working hard, as busy as a bee. That work, whether it be looking after your dad and Tahlia when your mum died or working at the orchard, helped you survive during your hardest times."

Pop put the next frame in the extractor and prepared the last one. When he was finished, he started the spinning.

"But, unlike the bees, you worked alone. That is until Beau came home."

I imagined the wax, capping and honey hitting the side of the extractor. What Pop said was true. Beau and I took daily walks through the orchard. We talked about the harvest, packing and everything else. Beau always helped with whatever I asked him to. He put his hand up for things before I asked. He'd taken over tasks.

"You would never trust anyone else with that. Like Beau wouldn't trust anyone else with his heart and mind."

Pop stopped the spinning and pulled the empty frames out. I placed a bucket with a strainer on top beneath the outlet. Pop opened it, and I watched the liquid ooze out. The wax and capping were caught in the strainer, and the honey dripped into the bucket beneath.

In all that time away, Beau hadn't had a relationship with anyone. That's what his mum had told Nan. He'd dated like I had. But all my relationships were on a shallow level. It was a bit of fun, interesting at times, but nothing lasting. It was nothing like what was possible.

"The bees wouldn't survive without each other. You and Beau might have survived apart, but you weren't really living."

It was time for us to start living.

CHAPTER TWENTY-THREE

Beau

20TH MAY. My birthday. I had some good birthday memories growing up, mostly with Clare. She saved my sanity on more than one occasion. Today would be no different.

"Happy birthday, Beau," Mum said as I entered the kitchen. Eggs and bacon were sitting on the counter with fresh Vienna loaf from the bakery.

"Thanks, Mum."

She came over to give me a kiss on the cheek.

"Do you want some help with breakfast?"

"No, no. Go sit with your father."

As I walked into the dining room, Dad looked up from the paper. "Happy birthday, son."

"Thanks, Dad."

"What has Clare got planned for you today?"

"She wouldn't tell me."

He nodded. He still held onto the paper, ready to resume reading at any moment. The doorbell rang. As I moved away to answer it, he did just that. Clare smiled at me as I opened the door. Her hair was a dusky pink today. It highlighted her warm brown eyes. She was in jeans and a thick jumper. Winter had a lot to answer for, hiding all of her delicious curves.

Clare stepped closer to me. "Happy birthday."

She wrapped her arms around my neck and leant in for a kiss. Kissing her was my new favourite pastime. I'm sure there would be other favourite pastimes too, but we hadn't made it that far yet. She pulled away too soon.

"Twenty-seven, huh? How's it feel to enter your late twenties?"

"I feel so much more like an adult...overnight."

"Yeah, right." She smiled over her shoulder as she headed down the hall; I watched her shapely legs the whole way.

The smell of bacon and toast filled the air as we entered the dining room. My stomach rumbled. Clare sat down at the place set opposite me. If we were at Nan and Pop's, they would have set our places right next to each other.

Dad put his newspaper down. "Got a big day planned?"

"I was going to take Beau to some pick-your-own farms, but none are in season now. I have something else just as good."

My heart swelled. If she were sitting next to me, I would squeeze her hand. We hadn't spoken much about our ideas in the last few weeks but to know she wanted to investigate mine was reassuring. She didn't think it was a worthless idea. That alone was a birthday present enough.

Mum brought the plates to the table. Dad and Clare's first. Then ours. My mouth watered at the smell of the bacon. It was crispy but not too crispy.

"Thanks, Mum."

Dad started eating straight away, and we followed suit.

Knives cut through bacon and clinked on the crockery beneath. The silence was oppressing. When I had children, I wanted the table to be full of chatter—inquisitive and fun chatter.

"We had a good harvest this year," Dad said.

Not just work chatter.

Clare nodded. "It was up on last year. The rain in spring didn't last as long this season, which helped."

"The bees would have liked that," I said. Bees were more active on dryer, warmer days. Active bees meant more pollination.

Clare's attention turned to me. "Pop said that too."

The work talk continued to the end of the meal. I sat in silence most of the time. Dad spoke mainly to Clare anyway.

"That was delicious, Sharon. Would you like help with the dishes?" Clare offered.

"No, dear. You and Beau head off. I can do them."

We stood up.

"Oh wait," Mum said, getting to her feet. "We haven't given you your present yet."

She rushed over to the kitchen bench and grabbed a wrapped gift. I opened it. It was a book on the history of apple farming in Tasmania.

"Thanks, Mum. This is great."

"It'll be good for you to see how our farms have evolved and how we are in the best state we've been in."

I turned the book over in my hands. Was she hinting at something?

"Thanks, Dad."

He nodded.

Clare and I made our way to her car. When we hopped in, she asked, "Is every meal like that?"

"Pretty much. Hasn't really changed since I was a kid." I looked back towards the house. "I wanted it to be different when I came back. I thought it might be, with how excited Mum was." I shrugged. What could I do? I'd tried to talk about other things, but the attempts were futile.

Clare let out a sigh. "No wonder you like eating at my place so much."

"That's not the only reason."

"Oh yeah?"

I cupped the back of her head and pulled her closer. My hand tangled in her short pink hair. "Yeah."

I skimmed my tongue across her full bottom lip. A hint of bacon teased my taste buds. Clare's hand rested on my leg as her mouth opened to mine. Her hand was close to my groin, and my dick knew it. Pressure built as it hardened and pressed against my zipper. Her hand moved closer. Clare's eager tongue met mine move for move. It would be so much better if we were in the back seat. Clare's hand left my thigh and covered my dick, rubbing it through my jeans. I moaned into her mouth. I opened my legs wider to give her better access. And she took it. She rubbed my whole length.

My breath hitched.

Her lips slowed. She pulled away, her hand still on my dick. Her chest rose and fell, keeping in time with my breaths.

She glanced out the window and removed her hand. My dick wanted to follow it. "I'm not sure having this much fun in your parents' driveway is such a great idea."

I reached down and adjusted myself. "No, it's not ideal."

"Your mum would have kittens."

I laughed. "If she didn't have a heart attack first."

Another thing for them to be disappointed about—the public display of affection. Or, more likely, it would be referred to as lewd acts in public.

Clare positioned herself back into the driver's seat and started the car. I adjusted myself again. She glanced down at my bulge, a small smile lifting her lips.

Things may not have been going to plan with my parents, but they were with Clare. This, what we had now, was exactly what I'd hoped for. I never wanted to be apart from her again.

CHAPTER TWENTY-FOUR

Clare

I TOOK hold of Beau's hand as we walked towards the building. The sign above the entrance said *The Bee Factory*.

"I'm sorry we didn't do this earlier when the pick-your-own farms were still open," I said.

His gaze landed on me. "You mean when you weren't speaking to me?"

Letting out a laugh, I said, "Yeah, then."

I looked down at our entwined hands. Four months ago, I would never have imagined speaking to Beau or liking Beau, let alone holding hands with him or kissing him. How did we get here? And where was here?

We spent more time together than apart—at home, at work, at Nan and Pop's. When we were apart, I missed him. Being with him was as natural as breathing. Our conversations flowed easily, like when we were kids. But was it too easy?

It had been easy all our lives, and he still left.

What was with his parents? They were happy he was

back, but it seemed like nothing had changed. It was like it had always been, like they didn't know how to interact with their own son. Like the only thing they had in common was work. Or the only thing they were interested in was work. Nan and Pop hadn't travelled widely, but they always managed to ask Beau questions about his time away. Or spoke about the environment. Or reminisced about their younger days. Or our younger days.

The automatic doors opened as we approached. The interior of the building was panelled in wood. It was warm and welcoming. I cast a sweeping glance around the space. There were all types of products for sale—honey, bee pollen, skin care and giftware.

"This is amazing," Beau said.

"Thank you," a middle-aged woman said as she approached. "My dad fell in love with bees fifty years ago. That's where this all started."

"You have a lot of varieties of honey," Beau said. "They're not all local."

She smiled. "No, we work closely with beekeepers all around Australia to source honey. The honeycomb, though, is all Tasmanian. It's illegal to transport honeycomb from other parts of Australia."

She led us to a window towards the back of the building. Acres of shrubs and gardens stretched before us. "In spring, we have flowers everywhere. To this day, my father still plants flower seeds to keep the bees happy."

I imagined the scene in front of us filled with colourful flowers. It would be Nan's dream. I needed to bring her here in spring.

"We have a working beehive that we show to visitors to explain to them how a hive works and how honey is produced. You should see the horror on some mums' faces when we tell them the queen bee has up to 60,000 children."

I laughed. "Bee children are much easier than human children."

The lady looked between us. "How many children do you have?"

My words stuck in my throat. Well, actually, I had no words.

"None yet," Beau said. *Yet?* "I'm thinking at least two. Being an only child sucks sometimes."

I don't think that was the only reason his childhood sucked.

"You're both young. You have plenty of time." The lady turned from the window and took us into a room with seats. At the end were glass windows with hives on the other side. Bees were intent and busy making honey. "This is where the hard work happens. Thousands of bees working hard to make food for themselves and us. The kids love it when we tell them that honey is made from nectar and bee spit."

"I bet," Beau said, laughing.

"Our live bee show isn't on for another couple of hours," she said. "I can see if I can find Dad if you like. He can talk you through the honey-making process."

Beau tore his eyes away from the bees. "No, it's OK. We have a hive at home."

She nodded.

"Do you also teach the visitors about the importance of bees to the environment?" I asked.

"Oh yes, Dad is passionate about letting kids know how bees help make the food they eat. And how without them, the world wouldn't survive."

Beau nodded. "Isn't that the truth."

The lady glanced between us. "I'll leave you to it. If you need any help, give me a call."

"Thank you for your time," I said.

Beau turned his attention back to the hive. The bees were moving, working their magic. Beau pointed to the queen bee, who was longer than the other bees. I looked closer and saw some boys. They were easy to recognise as they didn't have stingers.

"They have a great set-up here," I said.

"We couldn't compete with something like this, especially so close to home."

That was true, but I didn't want to give up on his and Pop's idea.

"I think we would need to niche down, maybe to apple honey," Beau said. He wasn't ready to give up either.

"We could still provide education, just not on this scale."

Beau turned to me. "Thank you for bringing me here. This is the best birthday present."

I smiled. It was the little things, like Beau being thankful for something so simple, that made him the person he was. He didn't take anything for granted, and that was special in today's world.

I didn't want to take him for granted. I didn't want him to leave again.

CHAPTER TWENTY-FIVE

Beau

CLARE and I walked into the conference room with Mum and Dad. They made a beeline for a small group of people. Clare and I followed.

"The man on the left owns a cider factory. One of the biggest in Tasmania. He started with his own orchard and now buys apples from other orchards," Clare said.

He was young, perhaps mid-thirties. When he spotted Clare, he gave her a wide smile. He glanced at me before turning his attention back to the group. I listened as Clare told me about the others in the group. All the while, Mr Cider kept glancing our way. He broke away from the group and approached us, giving Clare another smile.

"Ready to see if you can keep up with the boys again?" he asked her.

Keep up with the boys? He may have been older than us, but he still had a boyish charm about him—shaggy blonde hair and a smile with dimples.

"I think I've proved myself enough. You might need to

make your cider stronger so you can keep up with the big boys." She laughed, nudging him with her elbow.

He gave me a cursory glance. This was Clare's world, not mine. These people, their knowledge of each other, their friendliness, I wasn't part of it. I was like a drone bee kicked out of the hive. I spotted a table with tea and coffee. It would be the perfect excuse to get away, to let myself look in from the outside instead of being lost on the inside.

Clare took hold of my arm above my elbow. "This is Beau Hart. Beau, this is Clint."

He measured me up. His eyes paused on Clare's hand, still on me. He held out his hand. "Nice to meet you, Beau."

I took his hand, and he gripped mine tightly. His eye contact was direct.

"You too."

He held on longer than necessary before dropping my hand like it was covered in dung.

"Come and sit with us. We apple growers need to stick together."

"Actually, Beau and I are going to sit up the back. That way, we won't disturb anyone if we talk."

The slightest hint of a frown crossed his face. How many admirers was I going to have to deal with today?

I headed to the back with Clare. The conference was chock-full of information about the market, biosecurity, opportunities, solutions and technology. Clare's ideas encapsulated everything the conference covered. My stomach twisted with each new speaker. These ideas were the future. It was the way the industry was heading. My ideas were small-scale. They weren't about growing the business. They were about idealism, and idealism had no future.

And now my ideas were out there, soon to be judged by

Dad. Coming off the back of this conference, my ideas would sound weak. I took a deep breath. There was no point worrying about it now. I wouldn't let my anxiety win.

"The digital tools for managing labour, tracking productivity and monitoring soil conditions sound interesting," Clare said.

I nodded. "And not just for the orchard but the nursery too. The way it automates water and nutrient delivery was especially good."

The conference broke, and Mum and Dad made their way over.

"What did you think?" Dad said, pointing to the technology brochure in my hand.

"I liked what I saw. It has many useful dimensions."

Dad bobbed his head.

"I like the amount of control we have at the moment, but this takes analysing the data to the next level." Clare was excited as she flipped through the brochure.

"The fact that it can lead to lower costs is another selling point," I said.

"Yeah, because you only put in what's needed. There's no waste. And I like how it can monitor and forecast the harvest."

Technology might not mesh with my idea, especially seeing it would have to monitor different types of apple trees. I had to remember it wasn't about my ideas and whether Dad approved of them or not. This was about a sustainable future for the orchard.

Mum tapped Dad's arm to get his attention. "We're going for a walk before we get ready for dinner.

"OK. We'll meet you there," Clare said.

CLARE OPENED HER DOOR. The light from the hallway illuminated her silhouette as she stood there in a black dress that highlighted her deep red hair. It wasn't skin-tight, but it accentuated every curve of her body, especially her breasts. My stomach tightened, followed by my groin.

"You look nice," she said.

My black suit with crisp blue shirt paled in comparison to her.

I found my voice. "You're beautiful."

She blushed. "Thank you."

I closed the distance between us and pulled her to me. My lips found hers, and I kissed her softly. Her perfume was delicate and exotic, inviting me closer. My lips trailed her jaw to the spot directly below her ear, and I kissed with just enough force to make her quiver.

"I think we should stay here," I said.

"We need to go to the awards dinner." She made a futile attempt to step away. My hands held her firm. I kissed that tender spot again.

"Or we could feast on each other."

My hand dropped from the small of her back. Clare sighed, a small breath of pleasure escaping her mouth. Then she put her hands against my chest and pushed.

"Beau, we can't."

"We can."

Her lips were inviting me to kiss them again. My heart beat faster as I imagined kissing her lips, her body, all of her.

"Your parents are expecting us." She took a step away.

I leant in and held her there with the slightest touch, then whispered in her ear, "Let's see if you beg me to stop later."

She took hold of my hand and pulled me out the door. "We'll see."

I ran my hand through my hair. I needed to adjust the bulge in my pants.

The sooner we got back, the better.

CHAPTER TWENTY-SIX

Clare

We walked into the dining room, holding hands and waited to be seated. Beau was quiet beside me, scanning the room. Was he nervous?

I squeezed his hand. "What's wrong?"

He looked down at me and gave me a smile. A real smile. Nothing was wrong. "Just wondering how many men I'm going to have to fight off."

I laughed. "Um...none."

"We'll see."

I glanced at our joined hands. "It's pretty obvious we're here together."

"Sometimes men like a challenge, and another man's woman is as good as any."

"So, I'm your woman now, am I?"

Beau leant closer, his lips brushing my cheek. "Now and forever."

My stomach did that flippy thing I was becoming familiar with.

As if on cue, my name was called. I turned towards the voice but knew who it was before I saw him. Clint was coming towards us. His eyes were on me and me alone. I glanced at Beau and recognised his I-told-you-so look.

"Hey Clint, how are you?"

"Great. Yeah. The boys"—he looked towards a table—"and I wanted to check if you were up for drinks after dinner."

Not Beau and me, just me. Beau's stance didn't change. His hand didn't tighten on mine. He was putting on the best nonchalant act I'd ever seen.

"Actually, Beau and I have plans."

Clint's eyes flicked to Beau and back. "Yeah. Right. OK."

"Have a good night, Clint," Beau said, ending the conversation.

Clint walked back to his table. The waitress, who'd been standing off to the side, approached. "I can take you to your table now."

She headed straight towards Clint and his friends. I slowed down as much as I could without making it obvious and listened.

"—Beau Hart," Clint said.

"You may as well give up now," another man said.

"Why?"

"They've been into each other since we were kids."

"She hasn't dressed like that for the last five years."

"You have no chance."

"Just wait and see."

Beau would have heard them just as I had. He didn't flinch, didn't even look at them. He gave no indication that they existed. Not until we were out of earshot. "Looks like it's just the one I'm going to have a problem with."

We continued to our table. When we arrived, Sharon stood up. "Everyone, this is Clare, who you know, and our son, Beau."

Introductions were made, and Beau said a polite hello to everyone.

"What made you decide to travel?" one of the ladies asked.

Beau looked across the table, but before he could answer, Sharon said, "You know kids, they always want to see the world."

That was interesting. Did they at least acknowledge the real reason in private? They'd never wanted to before.

BEAU and I sat in the lounge room doing our homework. Tahlia was with Dad in the garden, reading her home reader to him. Mum and Sharon were sitting at the table having a cup of tea, talking about how Beau refused to ride to school without me.

"Maybe you should take Beau to talk to someone," Mum said.

Beau and I stopped writing and listened.

"There's nothing wrong with him. He was just being difficult," Sharon replied.

"He worries about a lot of things." Mum was using her quiet voice. The one she used when she wanted us to understand why something we'd done was wrong.

"Only because he doesn't want to do them."

I glanced at Beau. He was clutching his pencil.

"But there must be a reason."

"There is no reason. Like I said, he just likes being difficult."

Beau teared up. I touched my knee against his. We resumed our homework.

FROM THAT DAY ON, Mum made an extra effort to talk to Beau when something was worrying him. We spent more time at our place or Nan and Pop's, where we were free to roam the orchard.

The conversation at the table continued. Beau always thought I was the brave one, but I wasn't the one who'd left home and travelled the world. I'd stayed in little old Tasmania with everyone I knew.

"Clare and Beau have been working on plans to future-proof the business," Justin said, giving us a proud smile. I didn't imagine it, did I? He did smile at both of us, not just Beau?

"Is that so?" a grower Justin's age asked. "What have you come up with?"

Beau shifted in his seat. "We have a few ideas that we're going to present to Dad next week."

The announcer came on stage to tell us the order of the night. He mixed in some good old fruit jokes to get the audience warmed up.

Beau and I sat close together, sometimes holding hands, always touching. I swear the night was going in slow motion. The highlight came when Beau took his jacket off, and my mind went straight to his naked torso. When the night was over, I'd be seeing more than just his bare chest. A hot flush spread through me. I squeezed my legs together. Imagining a naked Beau in a room full of people was too much for a woman to bear.

I stood up. "I'm going to the ladies," I told Beau.

"I'll watch you every step of the way." It may have

sounded innocent to everyone else, but the slight huskiness in his voice told me he'd really be *watching* me.

I threw a glance over my shoulder as I neared the toilet. Beau gave me a lopsided smile. Flip. Dessert couldn't come fast enough. Maybe we could skip dessert and have each other instead.

A hand slipped round my arm and manoeuvred me to the doors that led to the garden.

"Hey gorgeous," Clint said, flashing me his best smile.

"Clint, if you don't mind, I was heading to the ladies."

I tried to extricate myself, but he held on tight.

"Come on, Clare. Let's get some alone time."

I stifled a groan and let him pull me through the doors, not wanting to make a scene in front of everyone. The door closed behind us, and he led me out onto the lawn, away from the lights.

"Clint, have you forgotten that I'm here with someone?"

"Beau." The name was said with such contempt I flinched. "I hear he dumped you eight years ago."

Is that what he thought? Is that what everyone thought?

"And what, now that he's back, you're a thing again?"

The door opened and closed silently. Beau stood in the shadows watching.

I pulled my arm away. "We're not a *thing*; we're a couple. And you need to respect that."

"I don't need to respect jack shit."

Clint reached for me. I stepped away.

"He'll just leave you again."

He won't.

"You don't know what you're talking about."

Beau strode across the lawn. Clint didn't see him coming. "I'm not going anywhere," he said, standing beside me. He took my hand. "Let's go back inside."

"She's too much woman for you," Clint said, blocking our path.

I wanted to smack him in his stupid face. But what would be the point? He was a loser.

"I know exactly how much of a woman she is." Beau moved me ahead of him. "You'll never know."

Clint was seething. We turned our backs on him and started to walk back to the door.

"If you throw that punch, it will prove what type of man you are," Beau said.

How did he know what Clint was thinking? And how was he so calm? I held his hand tighter

My body was tense, waiting, but the punch never came. Without so much of a glance back, we walked through the door. The announcer was presenting the awards. Beau walked me to the ladies room. Everything about him was controlled. He was always controlled, like when we'd been waiting to be seated. Clint's attitude hadn't antagonised him. I would've been furious, but he took it in his stride. Like Clint couldn't touch us or what we had.

"I'll wait out here," Beau said.

I took two steps and then turned back. I leant in close, my hands resting on his chest, unable to resist touching him. His calm display of masculinity was intoxicating. "I can't wait for you to show me how much of a man you are."

I walked away, then threw him a smile over my shoulder. "Oh wait, you already did. That was hot."

CHAPTER TWENTY-SEVEN

Beau

Clare walked into her hotel room, her dress moving across her arse with every step she took. My hands were itching to move across her whole body. I caught up to her and spun her around as the door closed behind us. Her hands clasped behind my neck as I kissed her hard and fast. The kiss wasn't the only thing that was hard. I pushed myself against her so she could feel exactly how hard I was.

I pulled my lips away from hers. There was way too much material between us. I took my jacket off and threw it in the direction of the chair. She pulled my shirt out of my pants and undid the buttons one by one. When the shirt fell open, she explored my stomach and chest with her warm fingers. My muscles tensed at her touch. Her fingers stopped on my tattoo, tracing it. Then she rested her hand over it and my heart. Could she feel how hard it was thumping?

"When did you get this?" she asked, her voice quiet.

"Five years ago. Even after three years of being apart, you were in my heart every day."

I reached down and tilted her chin up. I kissed her, slow and languid, my tongue searching out hers. Chocolate and ice cream danced across my taste buds. I pulled away, licking my lips.

"I could kiss you forever, but I have better things to do right now," I said.

I slid my fingers under the thin straps on her shoulders and slipped them off. My lips made their way to her neck, her shoulder and the top of her breast. The flesh there was so soft my lips sank in. Clare's breaths, the way they became louder but not yet a sigh, urged me on. I pulled the top of her dress down, so her breasts were exposed. I paused, taking them in, trying to memorise this moment and the way her nipples hardened before my eyes. I kissed one breast and then the other before taking each nipple in my mouth and sucking lightly. Clare sighed.

I reached down and pulled her dress up inch by inch until I could touch the bare skin of her leg. My hand went higher and higher. Her skin was soft. My dick was the opposite.

"I want to see how wet you are for me."

I slid my hand between her legs. Her panties were soaked.

I groaned. "Fuck."

My groin tightened. I needed every inch of me inside her.

Clare pulled my shirt off. Then she found my belt and slid it ever so slowly through the belt loops until it was free. She dropped it on the ground. She grabbed at the button of my slacks.

I took hold of her hand. "Not yet."

Her eyes widened. "What?"

I placed a finger over her lips and then reached behind her for the zip on her dress. I lowered it and pushed the dress down. It swished to the floor. I resumed kissing, starting at her neck and pausing at her breasts. Then I kissed lower. She trembled with every kiss. I stopped at the hem of her panties.

"You're not wet enough yet."

I dropped to my knees and licked along the hem. I held onto her legs, feeling the muscles spasm.

"You smell good."

I kissed the spot between her legs. She moaned.

"Beau, enough already." She attempted to pull me up.

"I haven't had nearly enough." I lowered her panties inch by inch. "I need to taste you."

She tried to pull me up again. "I thought I was in control of this relationship."

"You are, but I'm in control of the sex."

CHAPTER TWENTY-EIGHT

Clare

HOLY SMOKING DUCK SHIT. I was going to come before Beau's dick was anywhere near me.

"Beau, please."

He slid my panties all the way to the ground and then kissed up the inside of my legs. I wanted him so bad.

"Please, what?"

"I need you inside me."

He pushed me back towards the bed and onto it.

"I haven't tasted you yet."

He pushed my legs open and explored with his tongue. He twirled it around my entrance and dipped in. Then he licked until he reached my nub, sucking and teasing it. That was all it took. The sheets on the bed were so tight I couldn't grab them in my trembling hands. I clutched the throw instead as every part of me came undone. I cried out. Beau didn't stop until I lay spent before him, only tremors remaining.

"Now you're wet enough."

He kissed my thighs before standing up and dropping his pants. Never in my wildest dreams did I think Beau would turn into the perfect specimen of a man standing before me. His dick was hard and big. I scooted up the bed and watched as he took in every inch of me. My heart beat fast.

He rolled a condom on. How lucky that piece of rubber was. I licked my lips as he crawled up the bed and nestled between my legs. What was he waiting for?

"Beau?"

"Give me a sec. I want to last more than thirty seconds." He bit his lip.

Was he that turned on?

He slid in slowly and moaned. I wouldn't care if he lasted a minute. It felt so good. He started slow, taking his whole length out and then putting it back in.

He got faster. My hips met his thrust for thrust. He was holding his weight on his elbows. His arms shook.

"Oh fuck," he groaned out.

I pulled him down. His movements became harsher. I could feel every inch of him.

"Beau," I half whispered, half moaned.

His weight on me was glorious. He jerked as he came. His breath came in half gasps and grunts. I grabbed his shoulders as I clenched around him. Another shudder spread through him as I cried out. Kissing, sex—he was good at everything.

Beau withdrew and removed the condom before joining me under the covers. I rested my head on his arm, enjoying the warmth everywhere our bodies touched. The way he'd taken his time and explored my body was something to relish. I couldn't wait to do the same to him.

Six months ago, I'd wanted nothing to do with Beau, but

now I didn't think I could ever get enough of him. And it wasn't just about the sex or him being in control of it. I couldn't always be the boss.

I laughed. Sharing control was liberating.

"What are you laughing about?" Beau asked.

"The way you told me you're in control of the sex."

"And that's funny, why?"

"It's not funny, just ironic. I was in control of everything for so long and didn't know sharing it would be so good."

Beau pulled me closer. "I'm glad you lost control with me."

I grabbed his hand that was resting on his stomach and kissed it. "It could only be you."

He kept hold of my hand. "I'm sorry it took me so long."

He didn't need to be carrying that guilt around. It was what it was. "It doesn't matter. We're here now."

He nodded.

I wanted to know more about how we got here, how he'd battled his demons. I stared up at the ceiling.

"How did you know you were ready to come back?"

"My anxiety wasn't winning anymore. I wasn't fighting it every day."

"How did you make that happen?"

"Mike, my mental health support person, and I have been working on it for years."

"Mental health support person?"

Beau rolled onto his side to face me. "Yeah, sort of like an AA sponsor. He has training in mental health first aid. That's how our relationship started. But over the years, it changed into friendship."

I nodded.

"I've had my anxiety under control for a while, but every time I thought about coming back it flared up."

I couldn't imagine how that felt. Home was somewhere you should feel safe, like a sanctuary. He had to fight his anxiety for years. That was strength and determination. I moved closer to him.

"I take medication for my anxiety. It took a while to get the dose right. Sometimes I draw to keep my mind busy. I also go to the gym or exercise five times a week. Physical activity reduces stress." He took a deep breath.

"I think I can help with that," I said, giving him a nudge.

"I wouldn't say no." He kissed my temple. "You have my imagination on overdrive."

"Oh yeah?"

"The office, your bed, the kitchen bench. I'll need to write a list."

"The office, huh?"

"Yeah, the desks are sturdy enough."

"How would you know?"

"In my dreams, they are."

"Tell me more about your dreams."

"Just the sexual ones?"

CHAPTER TWENTY-NINE

Beau

Clare lay in my arms, her leg flung across mine. Light filtered in through the curtains and danced across my eyelids. I opened my eyes to find her watching me. She stretched up to kiss my jawline.

"I think we should skip breakfast downstairs and have room service instead." Her voice was clear like she'd been awake for a while.

"OK." I'd never say no to spending more time alone with her.

She smiled. I had everything I'd ever wanted. Mum and Dad appreciated me and my contribution to the business. They'd talked about it at dinner. But best of all, Clare wanted me.

"Text your parents. Tell them we'll meet them at the conference," Clare said, rolling onto her back and stretching as I watched her body. She was a goddess. My goddess. She sat up and swung her legs off the bed. "I'm going to have a shower. You should join me."

She walked to the bathroom. I sent a quick text and followed her. She was already in the shower, water cascading over her curves. I couldn't get in there fast enough. As soon as I did, I pulled her in close and kissed her. Water pooled between our chests before flowing over.

Clare reached down and took my dick in her hand. She held it firm, stroking. "Are you always this hard in the morning?"

"Only when I'm thinking about you."

"Mmmm, let's see how hard."

She licked the water off my neck and made her way lower, licking and sucking down my chest and stomach while her hand moved in a slow rhythm. My legs shook. I braced my hands on the shower wall to keep myself steady. Then her tongue licked around my head before she took me in her mouth. My dick throbbed.

"Oh fuck," I groaned.

Clare knelt before me, and I tensed my legs. Her head moved back and forth as she took me all the way into her mouth. She moved faster, faster. I splayed my fingers against the wall. She went faster again. She moaned, a satisfied sound. My stomach clenched. My body was on fire. A fire that was about to explode. She made the sound again. My balls clenched. And released.

"Clare," I groaned out as I exploded.

Her mouth came away, and she wrapped her hand around my dick. I emptied myself into her hand, cum and saliva mixed with the shower water. Clare licked. My legs spasmed. I cried out as my whole body shook. Clare didn't let go, pumping every last bit out of me. When my jerks subsided, she removed her hand. She moved her head closer as my dick began to soften. Then she licked me from shaft to tip, eliciting another shudder from me.

She rose slowly, her hands trailing up my body. I didn't move. I feared my legs would give out. My dick didn't know if it was finished or not as it jerked a few more times. But there was nothing left to give. Clare's wet mouth met mine, and she kissed me slowly, pressing her body against mine. I couldn't let go of the wall, not even to hold her close.

She pulled her lips away. "I think the shower is one of my new favourite places."

"It's at the top of my list."

"HOW WAS YOUR ROOM SERVICE?" Dad asked when we sat beside them.

"Good," I said.

The room service paled in comparison to the service I'd received from Clare.

Stop. This wasn't what I should be thinking about in front of my parents. I shifted from foot to foot, trying to ward off the hard-on that was threatening to grow in my pants.

"Delicious." Clare gave me a small smile.

The movement of her head. No, stop. Just stop.

I needed to change the subject.

"Clare and I are going to sit up the back again," I said.

Dad nodded. "Good idea. You can discuss how industry professionals envisage our future."

Was that a hint? No, not everything was about my ideas. I took a deep breath.

"Discuss how they align with your ideas."

Yep, that was a hint, alright. Another nudge saying my ideas had no future.

Mum and Dad moved away. Clint met them halfway

and then looked over at us, a sheepish smile on his face. He excused himself and headed our way. What now?

When he arrived in front of us, he looked down at his feet and then gave us a half smile. “Sorry I was such an arse last night.”

That was not what I was expecting.

“You went beyond arseholery,” Clare said.

He blew his cheeks out. “Yeah, I know.”

I couldn’t leave him hanging. I mean, I could, but he was man enough to apologise. I took hold of Clare’s hand. “No harm done. Maybe you should stick to cider.”

He gave me a grin. “Probably best.” He stuck out his hand, and I shook it. “If you’re ever in the area, you should drop in. I’ll shout you a couple.”

CHAPTER THIRTY

Clare

I STOPPED the car in Nan and Pop's driveway. Nan was at the clothesline getting the washing off. Dozer was at her feet, munching on a bone. He raised his head at the sound of my car. As soon as I opened the door, he came bounding over. We'd only been at the conference for two days, but he acted like it was a lifetime. I grabbed him up in my arms and hugged him as he squirmed and licked. He smelled bad, like he'd been rolling in blood and bone.

"Stop it," I said, putting him down and wiping my face. He ran between Nan and me. That dog had way too much energy.

"Hi, Nan," I said when I reached her. I started to help with the washing.

Nan looked at the car. "Where's Beau?"

"At home, getting dinner ready and spoiling Clementine."

Pop came out of the kitchen door. "Where's Beau?"

"Am I not enough for you?" I asked as I grabbed a singlet off the line and folded it.

"He's at home cooking," Nan said

"Home?" Pop examined me.

"Yeah. Home, you know, a place where people live." I grabbed a shirt off the line, ignoring the look Pop gave me.

"Rightio then, this sounds like a promising turn of events," Pop said and clapped his hands together. I couldn't help smiling at his reaction.

Dozer was rolling at Pop's feet. He was going to need a bath. I'd leave that to Beau.

"I think you should stop smiling," Pop said. "Anyone would think Beau makes you happy."

A cheeky grin appeared on Nan's face. "It wasn't that long ago she declared to us that Beau didn't make her happy."

I let out a breath. Those two might be old but they never missed a trick.

"Fine. You were right, as always. Everything feels like it's the way it should be."

"And Beau is here to stay," Nan said.

"Yes." Beau was here to stay.

Pop walked over to the clothesline to help. "Best you go grab Dozer's things. Can't keep that man of yours waiting."

"Thanks for looking after him."

"He's such a joy." Nan bent over to pat him.

"Tell Beau he has some repairs to do," Pop said. "I expect to see him soon."

"What repairs?"

"A fence to fix, a scarecrow to restuff, holes to fill in."

I shook my head and went to grab Dozer's stuff. He followed me every step of the way. When we got to the car,

I put him in the back seat and buckled him in. Without Beau to sit on, he'd wander all over the car.

Nan and Pop's reaction was like Sharon and Justin's—they were happy. Throughout the day, they'd spoken about how Beau and I had been working together for months now, and they were sure we'd take the business to the next level.

I glanced at Dozer in the mirror. He was looking out the windscreen.

"I don't think your dad was ever a threat to my job."

Dozer tilted his head.

"I needn't have worried."

Sharon and Justin wanted us to work together. And I'd thought they only wanted one of us. I turned the radio on and sang all the way home. When we got there, Beau came out to help.

"Your child needs a bath," I said as he unbuckled Dozer.

"My child? I thought this was an us thing?"

I grabbed Dozer's bag of toys. "I thought it'd be better for you to get in the bath with him. It might be easier."

"How do you figure that?"

"He likes being close to you. He might not be as scared."

"Yeah, OK. I'd rather him not be scared."

"Take him to the bathroom. I don't want him on the bed smelling like that."

Beau kissed the top of Dozer's head. "Don't listen to your mummy. You don't smell that bad."

Clementine met us at the back door. I put Dozer's bag down and picked her up. She purred in my arms and then stretched out to Dozer so they could touch noses. Contentedness spread through me. We shut the bathroom door behind us, and I put Clementine on the vanity and then filled the bath.

"I'm sorry," I said to Beau. "I can't make the water too warm because of Dozer."

"Another reason why this is a me job and not a you job." He stripped down to his t-shirt and jocks. That was disappointing. I was hoping to get a better view. I guess he was wary of being scratched. Beau hopped in, and I handed Dozer to him. Dozer was happy to lean against Beau and be washed.

"This is much easier," Beau said. "He's not even shaking."

Dozer reached up and licked Beau. Could life get any more perfect?

CHAPTER THIRTY-ONE

Beau

I REACHED out and switched off my alarm. Clare stayed still, probably pretending she hadn't heard it. I scooted closer to her and put my arm around her. Honey and almond from the shampoo she'd bought from *The Bee Factory* infiltrated my nostrils. She snuggled in. Leaving her on these cold winter mornings was becoming harder by the day.

"Do you want me to make you breakfast before I go to the gym?"

She wiggled her butt into my hard-on. "Maybe you could do your workout in bed."

I kissed her neck. "I think I could manage to do both."

She pressed against me again as I cupped her breast. "Mr Hart, I think that's a splendid idea."

"I bet you do."

I let my hand drift down and into her pyjama pants and underwear. I explored her wetness. She moved against my fingers. My dick couldn't wait to get out of my sleep shorts. But not yet. I slipped one finger in and then another. Clare opened her legs to give me better access. She moaned.

"Fuck, you turn me on." I slipped my fingers out and rubbed her hard nub.

"You're—" Her back arched. Her moan had my dick thumping in my pants.

I pulled her pants down and slipped in. No time for fun and games. Morning sex had to be quick sex. We'd already been late for work three times this week, and one of those days, I didn't even get to the gym. We couldn't be late today. Today was presentation day.

CLARE PULLED INTO THE CARPARK. I waited for her beside the door with her morning coffee. When she reached me, she gave me a kiss on the cheek before taking her cup and having a sip.

"Mmmm. Just what I needed."

"You know if our morning routine is too much for you..."

She leaned in and squeezed my arse. "Not even close."

"Good." I stepped away. "Ready?"

"Yes." She took hold of my hand. "Don't stress. We've worked hard on this."

It was true. The presentation was professional. We'd gathered all the data and figures. We'd used case studies and had spoken to people with the required knowledge and experience. My previous employers were more than happy to help. There was nothing left to do—except present it to Dad.

"I've set up the meeting room. Can you bring in the

printed presentations?" I asked her as we walked into the building.

"They're all ready to go. I'll meet you there in five minutes."

I walked up the stairs and looked at the floor below. It was quiet now that it was winter, and there wasn't any packing or sorting to be done. I took a deep breath. What would Dad think about our ideas? Clare's ran along the lines of what he'd be thinking. Mine would be something he hadn't considered. He was a straightforward-thinking man. My idea was far from straightforward.

It felt weird. It was like my idea was a part of me, and if he rejected it, he'd be rejecting me. I needed to separate the two. My ideas were a part of me, but they weren't me. Had he and Mum welcomed me back with open arms? Yes. But I always felt like something was missing. With Clare, it was the opposite. Our life was full.

I walked into the meeting room. Dad was already there. My heart rate picked up. I pressed my hand against my leg. It would be OK. We were prepared, and our ideas were well-researched.

"Good morning," I said.

Dad turned and smiled.

"I'll just set up. Clare will be here in a minute." I logged into the laptop and brought up the presentation. The silence was killing me. Where was Clare? When she walked in a moment later, my muscles relaxed.

"Hi, Justin." Clare handed him a printed presentation. He got a pen out of his pocket and opened the front page.

I clicked the button and started the presentation. Dad wrote a lot of notes as we went through the first half. Clare and I took turns talking. When we got to the second half, my half, Dad's notetaking all but stopped, and he squinted at the screen a lot.

"Well, that's it," Clare said after the last slide. "Do you have any questions?"

"Tell me more about the harvest platform you've chosen and why."

"Beau has experience in this area. Beau?"

"This platform is top of the line. It allows four workers to work at once, two on each side, on different levels. Everything is in front of the pickers. They pick and place the apples on the belt straight in front of them. So, no twisting."

"Right. Sounds good."

I sat down opposite Dad, and Clare sat beside me. We'd done our best to sell our ideas to him.

Dad looked at his notes. "Cherries are a good investment. They spoke about that at the conference. We still don't have enough growers to meet the needs of the market. The risk would be too many growers coming into the market."

"And buying and running another farm is a big investment," Clare said.

"Yes, a lot of our savings will need to be utilised, and a loan as well."

His face was neutral. Did he think it was too much risk to take? If he did, buying another apple orchard was probably out of the question too. He flicked through the printed presentation. He was silent.

"Did you have any questions about changing varieties?" Clare asked.

"Not really. We've done it often enough. It's achievable."

Did that mean he supported the idea? Did he even think it was a good idea? He gave nothing away. He closed the presentation and looked at us both. “Thanks for the presentation. Some good ideas here.”

Some good ideas, but not all.

“You two have your work cut out for you to choose one.”

Huh?

I glanced at Clare, whose eyes were wide.

“You want us to choose?” I asked.

“Well, they’re your ideas. You know them inside and out.”

“I thought you were going to choose,” Clare said.

“Wasn’t that the point? To future-proof the business for you?” I asked.

“Yes, but you’ve both worked hard. I think it should be your choice.” He stood up and put his pen in his pocket. “I’ll leave you to it.”

Clare and I sat in stunned silence for a few moments. Was this a test?

“I can’t believe he’s leaving such a big decision to us,” Clare said.

Neither could I.

“He seemed to favour two of your ideas. Perhaps that’s where we need to concentrate,” I said.

“I don’t know. It shouldn’t be just about making money. We should also think about leaving a better world for future generations.”

Dad may not have understood my vision, but Clare did. Clare always did. She did, didn’t she? Of course she did. Why was I even thinking she didn’t? Dad’s putting the decision in our hands had thrown me, that’s why.

CHAPTER THIRTY-TWO

Clare

Beau was still shaken about Justin's reaction to our presentation this morning. I didn't blame him. If Justin hadn't asked any questions about my ideas, I'd have been devastated. I would've thought my ideas were shit.

I didn't want to say anything to Beau about it. And we hadn't really had time to digest it together at work. I didn't want to make him feel worse. He'd told me once before that he'd left because he didn't feel worthy. His ideas not being respected would fall into that. Like that time his dad had dismissed his work on the science project. Would Beau leave again because of his dad's behaviour?

I stood in the kitchen and looked over at Beau on the couch with Dozer lying on his feet and Clementine lounging beside him. His brow wasn't creased anymore like it had been half the day. He looked worry-free. My muscles relaxed.

"Cream or ice cream with your apple pie?" I asked.

"Both."

"You'll need two gym sessions to work that off."

I put cream and ice cream on both serves. Beau glanced at our bowls when I sat beside him.

"And what are you going to do to work that off?"

"You," I said before popping the spoon in my mouth.

He handed me his bowl. "Have mine too."

I laughed. "You'll need all the energy you can get."

"Good point." He took the bowl back. "I'm not sure what to think about the presentation today."

I was totally unprepared. I didn't think Beau would want to discuss it. Maybe he was trying to decide if it was his anxiety or reality. He said that was something he'd do, and now he was choosing to do that with me.

"I was surprised he didn't ask many questions." I turned in my seat to face Beau so I'd be able to gauge his reaction better. "But it makes sense if he's not the one making the decision."

Beau nodded. "That's true."

"He hasn't been very clear through this whole thing," I said. "I wonder if us choosing was his plan the whole time."

"I don't think so. We weren't exactly talking to each other at the beginning. Us agreeing on something would have been near impossible."

"Yeah."

I ate my apple pie in silence. It was weird. Why would Justin ask us to make the decision?

"I don't know how we're going to choose," Beau said.

I'd been thinking the exact same thing. One of us would be disappointed. Beau's reaction was what worried me.

"I think we will need to set criteria and a scoring system," I said.

"Sounds like a good plan."

"You know what else sounds like a good plan?" I asked before I licked the bowl.

"You doing me?"

I leant over to give him a kiss. "Precisely."

"THIS PLACE IS SPECTACULAR," Beau said as we walked up a set of stairs at the Tahune Airwalk. Dozer was his usual happy self, checking everything out, smelling anything that looked interesting and saying hello to everyone we passed.

We could only walk single file along the metal walkway. The way it bounced with our weight was disconcerting. The gusts of wind moved the leaves and branches of the trees around us with such gusto the sound of our footsteps was drowned out.

I watched Beau and Dozer in front of me. Dozer kept looking over the side. He was obviously not afraid of heights seeing as we were thirty metres above the forest floor. Beau and I had agreed the night before that we wouldn't talk about work at home. I was happy with that decision. There was more to us than just Hart Apples. I hoped that if there was something bothering him, he would forget that agreement and be open with me. It was more important to me that we spoke about things rather than keep them to ourselves. I didn't want our relationship to be like one of the trees beside us—they stood tall and majestic until struck by lightning, devastated by bush fire or succumbing to old age, and they'd fall and crash into the trees below, breaking everything they came into contact with.

"Check out the leatherwood trees," Beau said as he stepped onto a wide platform.

I stood beside him, watching the trees sway in the wind. Their whole trunks swayed side by side. I marvelled at the roughness of the beautiful trunks.

"Pop said the trees don't get their first flowers for 150 years."

"Maybe that's why leatherwood honey has great medicinal value," Beau said.

"And why we need to protect them."

"And exactly why we need bees."

We stood close as we looked out at the forest surrounding us. Different trees had canopies at varying levels, some higher than us, some below us. Tree ferns were scattered on the forest floor. From up here, the fronds looked like flowers emerging from a bud.

We continued onto the cantilever. It was weird thinking that all that held us up, as we stood fifty metres above the river, were two thick wires. The sea of green from the trees was cut by the Huon River. Trees stretched all the way to the riverbank; the fact they found purchase there was surprising. The river flowed beneath us much faster than I expected. In the distance stood Pear Hill and Mount Picton. How long had this view existed? I could only hope Beau and I could last the test of time just like it.

CHAPTER THIRTY-THREE

Beau

"READY?" Dad asked as he walked into our office.

"Yep." I stood up and grabbed my water bottle. I followed him out. We were both wearing our navy Hart Apples shirts. He'd decided it would be a good idea if I went on a marketing run with him. He wanted me to learn all aspects of the business, not just the operational side.

"Where's our first stop?" I asked him.

"We've got a few fruit shops to visit first," he said as he hopped into the company ute.

"OK. Tell me more about them."

"The first is Hobart Market Place. They have a huge variety of fruit and vegetables. They've supported local growers for the past fifty years. They also offer a selection of Tasmanian gourmet food."

I googled them. I liked what I saw. A family business with eight outlets across Tasmania, they were big on relationships with growers and their customers.

"We'll visit two more similar outlets, both family-owned. The relationships I've built with them over the years stand strong today. They prefer to deal with farmers directly rather than through wholesalers."

"What about wholesalers? Do we have strong relationships with them too?"

"Yes, they help us get into the bigger supermarkets. Look them up."

He gave me the names, and I researched them while we drove. They dealt with supermarkets and hospitality. They boasted about their selection of local fruit and supporting farmers with the best produce in Australia.

"Will we be visiting restaurants as well?" I asked. I wanted to talk to them about heirloom apples and whether they'd be interested in what we could supply.

"We don't deal with restaurants directly."

That was disappointing but something we could change going forward, especially to showcase the gourmet aspects of heirloom apples. I wasn't sure if Dad would approve of me asking our customers about apples we didn't yet grow. But I couldn't know if it was a viable prospect without doing the research with our actual buyers.

"OK, this is our first stop," Dad said.

We parked in front of a grand building—a mixture of period and modern. I followed Dad inside and examined the amazing fresh produce on display, rows and rows of it. Dad said hello to all the workers we passed and stopped at a door at the back of the shop. He knocked.

A man in his sixties with short greying hair answered. "Justin, how are you?"

"Great, Bob. This is my son Beau. Beau, this is Bob. He's the general manager of Hobart Market Place."

I stuck out my hand for Bob to shake. "Nice to meet you."

"You too, Beau. Let me give you an introduction to our business." We walked around the marketplace, and I listened as he spoke about the history, the fruit and gourmet products he sold and their plans for the future. "I have four children. Two are working in the business. One runs his own store, and my daughter is the buying manager."

Like their website said, it was a family business.

"Is she available now? I'd like to ask her a few feasibility questions if possible." I hoped I wasn't being too forward. Dad's frown told me I was.

"Yes, come with me."

We walked into the office area, and he stopped at an open door. "Ingrid, do you have a few minutes to talk to Beau from Hart Apples?"

"Sure, send him in."

He ushered me in. And turned towards Dad inviting him in as well.

Dad shook his head. "Let's leave them to it. We can speak business."

They walked away. My ideas weren't business enough for him?

I glanced around the space. Ingrid was nothing like Clare. There were bookcases overflowing with books and folders. Same with her desk. Ingrid stood up, and I shook her hand.

"How can I help you, Beau?" She gestured to one of the seats, and I sat down.

"I'd like your opinion on something, please. We're thinking about diversifying our crop and planting some heirloom apples. Do you think there is a market for it?"

She sat opposite me, her hands joined together and pressed against her lips, considering me. I couldn't read her.

I planted my feet firmly on the floor; it didn't help stabilise my nerves.

"Beau Hart, I think you're a man ahead of your time."

Was that a good thing or a bad thing?

"A lot of our customers, in fact, our society, are looking at times past. They're seeking out old produce like purple carrots, figs and quince. It's a niche market that's growing in popularity."

"Is that something you could see your outlets stocking?"

"Without a doubt. I think you'll find it popular with chefs as well. The apples grown in the past hold their structure when cooked and have a unique flavour they can build gourmet meals around."

That was encouraging and exactly what I wanted to hear.

"It will take us a couple of years to grow a viable crop, and it wouldn't be large. We'd need to keep our commercial crop as well."

She nodded. "Makes sense. I think you'd have the best of both worlds—commercial to meet the needs of most consumers and niche to serve an emerging market." She handed her business card over. "I'd love to be on your list of buyers when you get started."

"Thank you, I'll let you know once we make a decision about varieties and timelines."

"Excellent."

I stood up. "Thank you for your time."

I felt light on my feet. Her confirmation of what I'd been thinking lifted me. My ideas weren't crazy. Diversification could bring success.

CLARE WATCHED me as I paced in front of the white-board. I couldn't stand still. I talked non-stop. "Everyone I spoke to said the same thing. They'd buy heirloom produce, and there's definitely a market for it."

"That's great." Her voice was flat.

My feet slowed. I scanned her face. She was frowning. My feet stopped altogether.

"You didn't think to discuss this with me before you approached our customers?"

"I didn't know the opportunity was going to arise."

"So, you didn't plan this ahead of time?" Her voice held a hint of anger and sarcasm. Why would I plan it without her?

"No. I took the chance when it was presented."

"It seems convenient to me." She crossed her arms.

"It was convenient but not in the way you're suggesting."

"You didn't plan to go behind my back?"

How could she accuse me of such a thing? "There was an opportunity. I took it. I didn't know I had to check in with you first."

Her jaw hardened as she stared at me. What was going on here? Her anger didn't make sense. We were partners in this. Asking questions didn't mean I was being under-handed. I mirrored her pose and gave the best Clare Stare I could muster.

"This isn't a competition, Clare. We need to make the best decision we can for the business."

Her stare softened. "You're right. It's about the business."

Even though she relinquished that fact, I was no longer feeling as confident as I had been.

CHAPTER THIRTY-FOUR

Clare

I NEEDED SOME TIME ALONE, so I headed to the treehouse. Beau's news had blindsided me. I don't know whether it was the fact that he didn't discuss his plans with me first, that he didn't tell me about it until he got back or that I wasn't included in any of it. Probably all three, to varying degrees. I sat against the wall and tucked my legs against my chest.

Footsteps approached and stopped. Pop must have sat on the seat below. "Do you want to talk about it? Whatever it is."

I stayed where I was and spoke loudly, telling him about the day—Beau speaking to our customers, his excitement, my reaction.

"Why do you feel betrayed?"

Betrayed, that was the right word, wasn't it? Anyone would think Beau had cheated on me from my reaction. All he'd done was ask our customers a few questions. I should be happy he'd had such a positive response.

"I don't know."

"Is it because he didn't ask you first?"

"I don't know."

That was so petty. Beau was a grown man and had made a decision. If the response to growing heritage apples was negative or positive, it was a response we needed to hear.

"It sounds stupid now. I think I was surprised that we didn't speak about it first."

"Maybe you should respect his effort at due diligence."

My stomach churned. Pop was right.

I moved to the opening and down the ladder so I could sit next to Pop. He put his arm around my shoulders.

"Relationships are hard work. Yours has had a lot of pressure early on."

I leant into him. "It's hard. I'm used to making all the decisions myself."

"And now Beau is making decisions too."

"Yeah."

"Do you trust him to make the right decisions?"

"Yes." Except for the possibility of him leaving. That worry still nagged at me. Would my reaction cause him to think about it? I really needed to consider my words. I had to stop thinking like this. He'd never given me any indication that he'd wanted to leave. Everything he said and did showed me he wanted to stay. I had no need to doubt him.

"If you trust him to make decisions, you need to tell him that."

BEAU WAS COOKING dinner when I got home. Dozer raised his head from the bed he was sharing with Clementine. I went into the kitchen and rested against the bench. I watched Beau from behind. His shoulders were set.

"Spag bol, your favourite," Beau said. He was extending an olive branch. He kept stirring and didn't turn around.

I shifted my feet. The ball was in my court. And Beau deserved for me to hit it straight back to him. "The info you collected today was good."

Beau continued to stir. "Thanks."

"I'm sorry about my reaction. It was wrong to accuse you of going behind my back."

His shoulders relaxed. He turned around and brought the spoon to me. "Taste OK?"

I blew on the sauce and tasted it. "Perfect."

"Friends in Italy taught me a few recipes. They treated me like part of the family and wanted to make sure I took their heritage with me wherever I went."

"What other recipes did they teach you?"

"Pasta puttanesca was my favourite. They even taught me how to make the pasta from scratch."

He went back to the stove and turned the heat down. "I didn't mean to go behind your back. I saw a chance, and I took it."

"I know. I know you wouldn't do that."

He stood in front of me and took hold of my hands. "Maybe I should have texted you throughout the day. I just got caught up."

"I would have too," I admitted. I wasn't lying. I wasn't saying it to appease him. "I don't know why I got so upset. It was stupid."

Beau smiled, a kind, gentle smile. "It's OK. I understand. Sometimes I get so caught up in my feelings I don't really think about what I'm saying."

I pulled Beau towards me. He lifted me onto the bench

and stood between my legs. I shimmied forward so I could feel him press right against me. His soft lips pried mine open gently, and his strong hands went around to the small of my back. Warmth spread from them and into my chest, melting my heart. As one hand went to the back of my head, his kiss deepened. His mouth pressed harder, and his tongue was more urgent.

And then the damn timer went off.

CHAPTER THIRTY-FIVE

Beau

"You're smiling. What's got you so happy?" Mike asked.

"Clare."

Mike moved closer to the screen. "What about Clare?"

Before I could answer, Lisa's face appeared on the screen. "What about Clare?"

"Things are working out. I've been staying there a lot."

Mike nodded. "I'm in awe of your patience, waiting for her to make a move. How's it going?"

"There have been a couple of hiccups. But I think we've worked our way through them."

"That's normal in relationships."

"Oh yeah, Mike and I have hiccups every day." Lisa poked him in the side.

"No, you and the kids have hiccups. I sort those hiccups out."

"I think you cause more than I do." Lisa turned to me. "So, have you moved in with Clare?"

"Sort of." I guess that's what you'd call it. I spent more time there than I did at my parents'.

"Oooh, big decision."

She disappeared when one of the kids called her.

"Now we have to make a huge decision together. We did our presentation, and then Dad said it was up to us to decide," I told Mike.

"You and Clare need to decide?"

I nodded. I hated the feeling of that weight on my shoulders. I didn't want to make a mistake that would negatively impact my parents' future.

"That's one way to learn to work together."

"It's adding some friction. That's what one of our disagreements was about."

"And you've worked through that?"

"Yes. We both recognised where we could have done better."

Mike smiled. "Beau, that's really good."

I couldn't agree more. Sometimes I wondered if Clare was holding something back, that she wasn't quite one hundred per cent there with me. But there was nothing in her actions I could pinpoint. It was just a feeling. Was it because it all felt too perfect, and I'd never had perfect before? Maybe I thought there were problems where they didn't exist.

"What hiccups did you have to deal with today?" I asked.

"Hudson decided to cut his sisters' hair."

"He cut both of their hair?"

"Oh yeah, they insisted. I reckon neither of them wanted to miss out."

"How bad is it?"

He swivelled his phone around. The two sisters were

sitting on the couch. I grimaced. It was bad, like Clementine bad. His face filled the screen again, and he smirked.

"The joy of having kids," he said. "How are your parents?"

He had to go there. I shrugged. He waited.

"They're happy I'm home."

"They were always happy that you were home."

Nothing got past him.

"Dad had nothing to say about my ideas in the presentation. And even after I got positive feedback from our customers, he didn't have anything to say."

"How did that make you feel?"

The way they always made me feel. But was it them or me? Sometimes I thought I was so sensitive to everything that no matter what they said or did, I'd feel the same.

"I felt deflated. That no matter what I do, it's not good enough."

"This won't fix itself. You need to speak to them, Beau."

"OK, well, we're having dinner in a few minutes. No time like the present."

"Talk soon."

I hung up and walked to the front door. It was the same suggestion every time. And every time, I dodged it. I thought that I'd learnt to accept myself years ago, that I was happy with who I was. Yet, I was still afraid of their thoughts. Why did it matter so much? I shrugged. There was no such thing in this world as unconditional love unless it came from a dog.

I needed to do this for myself. Enough hiding.

I went into the kitchen. Dad was at the dining table reading the paper. He folded it neatly and put it beside his plate. He'd likely go back to it as soon as dinner was over. I sat opposite him.

"How are things going with your decision?"

I held in a sigh. Did he have nothing else to talk about? I shouldn't think like that. It was important for the future of the farm and my parents. He was entitled to be curious. I just wish sometimes he'd ask about me or how I was first.

"We're finalising the details." I lied. We hadn't even discussed the criteria we were going to use yet. After our first heated discussion, we'd decided home time was our time. Our time to enjoy each other and our space, insulated from the rest of the world. Of course, we could have discussed it at work. We were both avoiding it, and that wasn't wise. We needed to get it over and done with so we could move on.

How was I going to ask the questions rolling around in my head? The ones that had been pressing in on me since I'd returned. Mum started plating up dinner—steak and three veg, like always.

Well, if he wanted to talk about work, let's do it. "You didn't have much to say about my ideas in the presentation."

Dad stared at me. I stared right back. Mum brought our plates over.

"They were good ideas. You put a lot of thought into them."

Amazing. Something positive.

"I'm glad to hear that. I think I would have liked to have heard that on the day."

Those were antagonising words, and I knew it. Why did I have to be so defensive?

"I said there were good ideas. I asked the questions I wanted to ask."

Mum sat down next to Dad. "Your ideas were good, Beau."

I nodded. This was going nowhere. I cut my meat and

concentrated on chewing it. I needed another approach. I could turn it around on myself and use the 'I feel' strategy.

"I feel that things have been strained since I came back."

I left the comment out there for them to reply to. They didn't. My heart dropped.

I took a deep breath and ploughed on. "When I was a kid, I always felt like I was a disappointment to you. I didn't want what you wanted. And that made me feel guilty and anxious."

I broke out into a sweat. I placed my cutlery down and wiped my sweaty palms on my jeans.

"It is a disappointment when your only child doesn't want to follow in the family business," Dad said.

Finally, some truth.

"Just because we were disappointed, it didn't mean we didn't love you," Mum said. She looked at Dad, expecting him to back her up. Nothing.

"I know you love me, Mum."

We ate in silence for a while. I moved on to my vegetables, leaving a last bit of steak to enjoy at the end.

"Are you still disappointed?"

"Well, you're back now," Dad said.

That wasn't an answer. I took a sip of my orange juice. Was I ever going to get the answers I wanted?

"Your ideas aren't ones I would have considered to make a business sustainable."

"But Clare's are?"

"Yes, she has a good business head."

I guess that meant I didn't.

Dad stopped cutting his steak. "Look, Beau, you're back after eight years. I wonder if this is just another phase in you *finding yourself*."

Because me getting away and removing myself from the pressure I felt, trying to find a way to be happy, was a bad thing. I didn't think like him or Clare, and that was a bad thing. I wasn't like my parents and didn't want the same things as them, and that was a bad thing. Yes, I wanted to improve the business, but not in the way he envisioned. Everything about me was bad.

I'd come into this dinner with questions about being enough for my parents. They didn't outright say I wasn't. But they'd said enough.

My stomach turned. I didn't want to discuss it anymore. They'd never understand how I felt. To them, my feelings were irrelevant. I ate the rest of my dinner in silence. The food tasted like cardboard, and I forced it down. Every mouthful was harder to swallow.

"You should donate my clothes."

Mum looked at me sharply.

"There's no point hanging onto them. That boy has gone now."

What made me say it? Maybe I wanted them to think about how I'd changed. Even though, to them, I hadn't changed at all.

Mum's eyes averted to her food, and she resumed eating. Thirty-two chews for every mouthful. The memory of her voice reminding me I couldn't even eat properly.

Getting back to Clare would be a relief.

CHAPTER THIRTY-SIX

Clare

It was strange having dinner alone. And being the only one to share my food with Dozer and Clementine emptied my plate faster than usual.

"How was dinner?" I asked, looking up from the TV as Beau entered the lounge room.

"OK." Beau walked to the fire and stood in front of it. He shrugged. "I asked them what they thought about my business ideas."

My heart sped up. There was a rift between Beau and his parents that never seemed to heal. It's not like they had rip-roaring arguments; it was silent turmoil built around acceptance or lack of it.

"And?" The answer wasn't going to be good.

"Basically, they don't line up with Dad's vision, and I don't think like a businessman."

"Oh." What was I supposed to say to that?

"Dad thinks my returning is just another phase I'm going through."

I sucked in a breath. "It's not an unreasonable thought."

His head snapped up. "What?"

Shit.

My big mouth needed to shut up and let my brain think before it spoke. I was about to say I was sorry, but I wasn't really. I might have been sorry about not sugarcoating it. But I didn't regret the message.

"I think you need to see it from their perspective." I better not dig myself a deeper hole. Think and then speak. "You've been away for eight years. It will take time for them to trust that you're back here for good."

"I've said I am."

"But words can be empty words."

Beau's eyes narrowed. Oh crap, I should have found a better way of saying it.

"Right, so I left before, and I'll leave again. Is that it?"

I moved forward to sit on the edge of the couch. What was the point of lying?

"It's possible."

"So, you agree with my parents?"

I looked up at him. The height difference was intimidating. I stood up.

"I'm not going to lie, Beau. You leaving is one of my greatest fears." My heart hammered in my chest.

He stared at me and shook his head. "These last few months haven't all been a piece of piss. I could have left any time. It's not like I haven't had job offers."

"What job offers?"

"It doesn't matter. The fact is I chose to stay."

But it did matter. A job offer was more than he had the last time he'd left. And the fact he'd never told me also mattered. Why would he hide it unless it was a safety net for him?

"So, you thought about leaving?"

He fisted his hands. "No, Clare, I didn't think about leaving. I never want to leave you again."

I closed my eyes. I wanted to believe his words.

He let out a sharp breath. "Don't you get it? My place is with you. I love you."

He said he loved me. I was way past love. What was past love? I don't know. To me, he was what a queen bee was to her hive—without her, it would collapse. Without Beau, my heart would collapse.

"I love you too."

Beau strode over to where I stood and embraced me. I was torn between his words and my fears. I knew what eight years without Beau was like, and that was before I loved him completely. It was before I knew I loved him. If he left again...

I pushed the thought away. What was the point of being with him if I didn't trust him? I needed to trust that he was not like an absconding bee that would leave at the first sign of discomfort and that our love was strong enough to keep him with me.

Beau kissed the top of my head. "We need to be more open with each other. If we can't tell each other our greatest fears, how can we truly say we love each other?"

He was right. Nan and Pop knew each other intimately. That's because they'd been through hard times. Not just been through them together but supported each other through them. They believed in each other.

I needed to believe in Beau.

CHAPTER THIRTY-SEVEN

Beau

THE OFFICE WAS quiet without Clare. She was down at the nursery, checking the stock. She'd been there all afternoon. Being alone gave me a lot of time to think, and thinking was not good. The pain I had caused her when I'd left kept coming back to haunt me. It was something I'd had to do, but it had harmed my relationships. That wasn't something I had considered when I'd left. She didn't trust me to stay, neither did my parents.

There was a knock on the door. Mum stood there, hesitating in the doorway.

"I'm sorry about how dinner went the other night," she said.

"I think it's good that it's all out in the open." Although not everything was. Not my mental illness. It was something I had to keep hidden like it was a dirty secret.

She gave me a small smile. "When you said you were coming back, we thought about how to make the transition easier. That's why we teamed you up with Clare. We thought she could help you find your place."

It was some sort of master plan?

"Clare did an amazing job helping you. We're so proud."

"Yes, it worked out great."

"We knew it would. She was always such a good influence on you."

What was she trying to say? I was too useless to make it on my own?

"Oh yeah, I couldn't have got through it without her."

She nodded, obviously happy with herself. "Have a good night, Beau."

How much of this did Clare know about? Was she a spy feeding info back to my parents? How frustrating it must have been for them all when I wasn't influenced by her business acumen. What it boiled down to was that none of them trusted me. They didn't think I could do this on my own. And what was it they wanted me to do exactly? Stay for starters. Run the business? Definitely not. They'd designed everything so Clare was with me every step of the way with her *business brain*.

Did she even believe in my ideas? She probably thought they were crap, not business-y enough for her. Stop. Truth or anxiety? Probably anxiety. Maybe. I clenched my teeth so hard my jaw hurt.

I stood up and switched off the computer. I needed to get out of there and away from them all. I couldn't stop thinking of their duplicity all the way home. It wasn't even my home. It was Clare's.

Dozer came running up to the gate when I pulled up. At least I knew his love for me was real. He had no ulterior motives.

"Do you want to go on a trip?" I asked him as I entered the backyard.

He jumped and ran around me.

"I'll take that as a yes."

I went inside and packed quickly. I needed to get out of there before Clare got home. I couldn't face her. Not until I got my thoughts in order.

I left her a note and drove off in the opposite direction to where she'd be coming from. I couldn't so much as look at her, not until I sorted out my thoughts. I pulled into a parking bay on the side of the road and searched for somewhere to stay for a couple of days. All I needed was a place for Dozer and me. It didn't need to be anything fancy. I chose the first place that came up on the booking site.

I'd tried to clear my mind on the drive, but it had been pointless. They thought I needed help to find my place. I'd worked around the world in places they'd never even dreamed about. I'd found my place there with people who respected me, people I considered family and still kept in contact with. They didn't question everything I did. They listened to me as their equal. They treated me kindly. And even now, they invited me back.

And yet these people who *were* my family, who said they loved me, couldn't treat me with the same respect. I was home, but was I really?

How much of this did Clare know? Was she in on it from the beginning? Is that why she resented me so much when I came back? Because she had to babysit me and help me find a place where she belonged more than I did?

She must have known. She and my parents were close and had worked together for seven long years. Dad trusted her implicitly. This plan of theirs explained why she was so angry. First, the man she hated came back and then she had to play a part in their plan to amalgamate him back into the business.

I was so swept up in trying to recreate what Clare and I had I'd missed all the signs—how she'd given Dad the death stare when he moved me into her office, how she hardly let me out of her sight, her bitterness when I'd gone out on the marketing run. She'd already future-proofed the business; she didn't need my juvenile ideas.

She didn't need me.

The key to the holiday house was left in the door for me. Thank goodness I didn't have to meet anyone. I wouldn't be able to offer any pleasantries, let alone hold a conversation.

I needed time to think this out.

Alone.

CHAPTER THIRTY-EIGHT

Clare

Beau's car wasn't in the driveway, and Dozer wasn't in the backyard. Maybe they'd gone to the dog park. It was one of Dozer's favourite places. That dog was a blessing in more ways than one. I'd always attribute breaking down the walls between Beau and me to that dog.

I dumped my bag in the lounge room and went to the kitchen to start dinner. There was a note on the bench.

Dozer and I are going away for the weekend. Be back Sunday. Beau.

My heart dropped.

I stared at the note and reread it. Why would he go away? Was he still upset about his parents? I thought we'd worked through that. I'd been open about being scared he would leave, and now he'd done just that. A weekend wasn't forever...but it was enough.

I looked at the note again. He didn't even sign it 'love Beau.' Just 'Beau.'

This was stupid. I was reading too much into it.

I left the note on the bench and went to shower. I didn't feel like eating anymore. I stood under the hot water rushing over my body, not wanting to go back out into the empty space.

I needed to check that he was OK. Something wasn't right. The warm water suddenly didn't feel warm enough. He'd wanted to take his own life once before. He didn't feel like that again, did he? His mood had changed over the past couple of days. He'd been lost in thought more often and wasn't quick to register when I was talking to him.

I didn't know much about anxiety, only what I'd seen with him when we were younger. Maybe I could speak to Pop, but I didn't want him and Nan to worry. Maybe I was overthinking this. Maybe this is what people did when they were feeling overwhelmed and needed a break.

I hopped out of the shower and dried myself quickly. The bathroom was hot and toasty from the steam and heat lamps, but it was winter in Tasmania, and the air wouldn't take long to cool.

I checked the medicine cabinet. His medication was gone. That was a good sign., wasn't it?

If I texted him, would he think I was checking up on him because I didn't trust him? But if I didn't text, would he think I didn't care? I gritted my teeth. He needed to know I cared, damn it.

Are you OK?

I sat on the couch and waited for the three dots to appear. Nothing. Was he OK? I wouldn't even know where to start looking. My knee bounced.

I needed to speak to someone. He had a friend he talked to who was once his mental health support person, but I didn't know his contact details. All I knew was that his name was Mike. And he had a wife. Four kids. Two cats. And a rat. But I had no idea how to contact him.

I called Tahlia instead.

"Hello." Her voice was cheery.

"Hi, Tahlia."

"What's up?" Obviously, my response wasn't normal. Usually, we pushed on with what we were going to talk about without the hellos.

"I got home and found a note from Beau telling me he's gone away for the weekend."

"Where's he gone?"

"I don't know. He didn't say. I'm worried."

"Have you tried ringing him?"

"I texted to ask if he was OK. He hasn't responded."

"Maybe he's out of range or doesn't have his phone with him. I'm sure he's fine."

I shrugged. "Maybe."

"Did you two have a fight?"

"I guess you could call it that, but that was days ago."

"What about?"

"It started with him visiting some customers in Hobart and asking them questions about his idea."

"And?"

"I thought he was going behind my back."

"You said that to him?" Her voice was incredulous.

"Well, yeah. Sort of, yes."

"I assume he didn't take that well."

"No."

It's the way I'd felt at the time. I wasn't going to change my feelings. Even now, his actions felt a little traitorous. Jeez, that was stupid. I needed to let it go. He'd done nothing wrong.

"And then what happened?" Tahlia prompted.

“We smoothed it over.”

But had we? I still felt this tiny bit of resentment. He’d said it wasn’t a competition, and he was right. I should have let it go.

“If you smoothed it over, why would he leave?”

I stared up at the ceiling. “I don’t know.”

I did know.

“Did something else happen?”

“He had dinner with his parents, and when he came back he was in a funk. They weren’t very nice to him.” Neither was I. “I tried to tell him he should see it from their perspective.”

“See what from their perspective?”

“That it was reasonable for them to think he might leave again.”

It sounded horrible. I was so horrible.

“Clare.” Her disappointment hit me hard. “You didn’t tell him you felt the same, did you?”

“There was no point lying.”

The phone buzzed in my hand. A text from Beau.

Yes

I sank back into the couch cushions and let out a sigh of relief.

“He just texted. He’s OK.”

“That’s good.”

I nodded even though she couldn’t see me.

“Let’s get back to the other subject. What did you say to him?”

I didn’t need to think about my answer. But the way she put it had me on edge. Why was I the one in the wrong?

“He’s done exactly what I was thinking. He left.”

“For the weekend.”

"But what about next time?" A cold chill spread over me.

"There doesn't need to be a next time."

I suppose not. Maybe. Or maybe he'd take one of those mysterious job offers and go somewhere he could be happier.

How was I going to face him when he returned when all I could think about was him leaving?

CHAPTER THIRTY-NINE

Beau

I PULLED into Clare's driveway. Two days ago, I would have said our driveway. Two days had passed, and my thoughts were no clearer.

I didn't want to go back. No, I did want to. I loved Clare and the family unit we'd made for ourselves in such a short time. I wanted it to work. But her doubt, and that of my parents, was working against me. Any belief I'd had in myself six months ago had eroded. I no longer believed I was able to contribute to the business in a positive way. I no longer believed my ideas were good. Not that I'd completely believed they were in the first place, but they were important to me.

I couldn't decipher what was true and what wasn't. Clare's support for my ideas could have been fake. Her taking me to The Bee Factory was her way of showing me that my ideas weren't original and that they wouldn't work at Hart Apples. Maybe her love wasn't as true as mine. I could have been holding onto a childhood love that couldn't grow into an adult love. I'd just latched onto her because of those feelings.

And then she didn't think I was going to stay. There was no way she could love a person she doubted. She and my parents must have been speaking about it behind my back because they all thought the same thing.

When my thoughts started to spiral out of control like this, I began to wonder if any of it was real. Maybe life was just some weird dreamscape where I'd live eternally in despair. I never seized on that thought, though. It was only fleeting. I knew everything was real, and there was no escaping it.

I needed to talk to Mike to get clarity. My stomach twisted. I was twenty-seven years old and couldn't even deal with my own crisis. It was fucking stupid. But still, he'd help me make sense of it. Just two more days until our monthly phone call. I needed to keep it together for two more days. Surely even I could manage to do that.

I ran my hand over my face and opened the back door. Dozer ran into the laundry. His whole body wagged as he waited for me to open the door to the rest of the house. As soon as I did, he raced down the hallway. I followed at a slower pace.

Dozer was up on the couch receiving vigorous pats from Clare. I was relieved that the focus wasn't on me. I took my bag to the bedroom before going out to the lounge room. Clementine was sitting beside the couch. I picked her up and stroked her crazy fur, using her as a shield to protect myself. I stood in front of the fire and looked at Clare. I broke out into a cold sweat.

"Did you have a good weekend?" she asked, her voice tense.

"Yes, did you?"

"It was alright."

Is this what it was going to be like? We were like two strangers sharing pleasantries.

"Where did you go?"

"I found a house to rent near the beach."

"That sounds nice."

Pleasantries. Polite but separate. No bee colony here, sharing space or working together. We weren't a single, functioning being.

"Have you had dinner?" I asked.

"I had some toast." She continued to pat Dozer, but it was much more subdued.

I nodded. I didn't feel hungry. Stress could do that to a person.

"Mum and Dad are coming in for a meeting tomorrow."

"OK."

I stood. She sat. We said nothing.

"I'm going to bed." I put Clementine down and left them all there.

MUM AND DAD were waiting in the meeting room when we arrived. Keeping my shit together was impossible by the time I walked in there. I was ready to have it out with all of them. It didn't matter if it was a good idea or not. I tried to stop shaking, but it was hopeless.

Mum and Dad sat on one side of the table and Clare on the other. I chose a seat as far away from all of them as possible. I anchored myself to it, clenching my whole body.

"When I came back, I came back with the hope of fitting back in." I didn't have the energy for any preamble.

Mum's jaw set as soon as the words were out. She must

have thought her little apology the other day was enough. Not even close.

"I'd worked hard for the past eight years in the industry, learning what I could. I hoped it would prove useful when I came back."

Clare turned to me and opened her mouth as if to speak.

I banged my hand against the hard wooden desk and gave her a hard stare. "I'm not finished yet."

Her eyes widened as she closed her mouth.

"I'd proved myself in other places. I'd earnt the respect of those I worked with. I knew I had to prove myself to all of you the same way I did with them."

I looked at each of them to make sure they were listening. Shit. My heart thumped as their faces stared back at me. My breathing was shallow.

"I did everything you asked of me. You didn't respect my ideas, but I persevered." I peered at Mum and Dad. "From the start, it was obvious you didn't approve of them." I turned to Clare. "But you pretended there was some value to them. I thought you believed in me."

Clare's mouth dropped open.

My fists were clenched under the table.

"None of you believed. You didn't believe in me or my ideas."

Dad went to speak.

"Then you decided to make Clare and me choose which idea we should implement. Why? Because you were too piss weak to say no to me. I would have gotten over it. It's your business. You can do what you like."

Dad shook his head.

"Don't bother. I don't want to implement my ideas here.

Go with Clare's. I suggest you purchase a harvester. It's the lowest investment but will yield the best returns."

I was struggling not to stand. My voice broke. "Your plan for Clare to team up with me so she could 'transition' me back into the business worked a treat."

Clare's head swivelled between us. "What?"

I stared at her. "Sorry I didn't play my part to perfection and learn your superior business ways."

Mum sat up straight. "Beau—"

"What? Have I missed something?" I tilted my head at her. "I've spoken about believing in me, respect, your skilful plot with Clare...Oh, that's right, you all believe I'm going to leave. Isn't that right, Clare?"

CHAPTER FORTY

Clare

I WAS ABOUT two minutes behind in the conversation. Beau was so angry it was hard for me to grasp his words. I tried to catch up, but my brain wouldn't move.

"What plan are you talking about?"

"The plan where you were babysitting me, helping me settle into the business. Who knows what else."

Justin's face was red. Sharon shifted in her chair. "Clare, darling, it's not what it sounds like."

My hands were shaking.

"Beau is blowing it all out of proportion," Sharon said.

What the fuck was going on? None of this made sense.

"How about you put it in proportion then?" I said tersely.

I looked at Justin first, offering him a chance to speak. "It isn't what Beau is thinking. You two were always close. We just thought it would help Beau fit back in if he worked with you."

I turned my eyes to Sharon.

"We didn't *plan* it out like Beau is saying. We thought it would be hard for him, and you'd make it easier."

I'd make it easier? For them. I'd made it easier for them.

"You know what would have made it easier? Being honest. Telling Beau how you felt. That would have made it easier."

I knew I shouldn't have trusted them. My job had never been secure once Beau had returned.

Sharon was crying. "There was nothing sinister about it. I just didn't want to lose him again."

She couldn't even fucking apologise.

It was all about keeping him. They would have gotten rid of me in a split second if it would keep him.

"If Beau said he didn't want me here, you would have made that happen, wouldn't you?"

Sharon looked down at the desk.

"I gave you my all for the past seven years. I tried everything to improve the business. Did that mean nothing to you?"

Justin spoke up. "Of course, it did. That's why we teamed you up with Beau because you know more about this business than anyone else."

It made sense; I knew it did. If they'd hired an assistant manager, I would have been the one to show them the ropes. But it was the fact that when I'd asked about choosing Beau over me, Sharon couldn't answer me. She'd choose her son. I mean, who wouldn't? But she couldn't even say sorry or try to explain herself or try to make me feel better about the whole thing.

I clenched my fists. Fuck this. That whole speech from Beau alluded to him wanting to leave, to leave me. He wanted to go where he was welcome. Fuck that. I'd finish that delusion for him. "Well, it's lucky that Beau is going to stay, which means you don't need to choose between us." I glared at Beau and at them. "But I'm not staying."

I stormed out. I went into my office and grabbed what was mine, shoving it into my backpack any way it would fit. The pens rolled off my notebook and clattered onto the desk. Not my desk, nothing here was mine anymore. The stupid ideas on the board stared down at me, mocking me. I shoved things into my backpack with such force the computer screen shook. If my hands stopped moving, they would shake too.

We didn't want to lose him. We thought you'd help him fit back in. Who cares if you feel used and abused? I was stupid. So fucking stupid.

And Beau? How could he think I would deceive him like that?

Beau came in. I threw the backpack over my shoulder. He was lucky I didn't smash him over the head with it.

"Clare—"

"Fuck off, Beau. I don't need to hear any more of your shit today."

"I—"

"I'm sorry you're stuck here." I couldn't hold in my contempt. It ate at me. "Shame you can't run away, seeing you're so good at it."

Beau frowned. I hope those words hit him where it hurt most.

I pushed past him. "Text me before you come and collect your things. I'll make sure I'm not there."

I stormed down the stairs. Arsehole. I turned back and saw him standing at the top. I sneered up at him. "Have *fun* with your parents."

Then I turned and went down the last few steps.

"Clare, wait," Justin called after me.

The door didn't seem to get any closer, no matter how fast I walked. I looked straight at it. The shed was suffocating me. As soon as I reached it, I thrust it open and hurried through. The crisp air enveloped me. I sucked in a breath. Nausea threatened to take over. My head was spinning. My whole life was careening out of control.

My car. I needed to get in it. I needed to get far away from this place, away from them. I yanked the door open and flung my bag onto the passenger seat. There was no time to dawdle. I drove out of the orchard, gripping the steering wheel to stop my hands from shaking. The tears started slowly and then engulfed me.

They'd used me to get to Beau, and, what was worse, he believed I was in on it. His anxiety could have caused that, but he'd delivered the message with a final blow. He knew exactly what he was doing when he accused me of conspiring with them.

He lumped me in with them. He said I didn't believe in his ideas or in him. But I did. I had doubts about him staying at first, but I'd worked on them.

My throat hurt as I tried to stop the tears, but I couldn't. I cried all the way home.

Dozer was at the gate waiting for me. My heart tore in two. I bent down and patted him. He didn't run around like crazy but trotted beside me, watching me, as I went to the back step. I sat down and pulled him into my lap. Sinking my face into his fur, I held him tight. My beautiful Dozer. This would be our last moment together. I'd never see him again. I stroked his soft ears.

"I love you, boy."

I nuzzled his face; the cute face so full of expression. Tears and snot ran into each other.

"You're such a good boy."

He licked my face. I kissed him.

I'd lost both of them.

Dozer and I sat there until the text came. Then I put him on the ground and walked away.

CHAPTER FORTY-ONE

Beau

I SAT in the office with the door closed. This was the second day without Clare, and it was worse than the first. I'd rubbed all the ideas off the board yesterday, but I could still see the words, fainter, almost indistinguishable, haunting me.

What the fuck had I done? The look on Clare's face as she'd turned as white as apple flesh, her wide eyes, and her angry words, kept spinning around in my head.

She was gone. I did that.

Someone knocked on the door. I ignored them. It was too late for talking. If they needed to discuss business, they could email me. I'd fulfil my duty, but that was it. I stared at the screen. It was pointless being here in my non-functioning state. But I couldn't leave until I knew the person who'd knocked had gone.

The silence was a creator of thoughts, and thoughts were not what I needed. My anxiety crept in and took hold.

I ran my hand through my hair.

"You need to explain that."

"She didn't defend my ideas. I felt like she thought they were crap as well."

"Did she say that? Or did your anxiety say that?"

I swallowed. "Probably my anxiety." I searched the room for Dozer. He was asleep on my bed. "And it wasn't just that. She also told me she was scared I was going to leave again."

Mike moved in his seat, and his face came closer to the camera. "I don't think that's surprising."

"I know, but the idea that she didn't trust me got me thinking and doubting."

"Beau, we've discussed this before, the way you struggle to get past things. Your anxiety feeds on these moments. Clare opening up and telling you that must have been hard for her."

Tears sprung to my eyes. She trusted me enough to tell me her greatest fear, and I threw that trust away.

"I assume there's more."

I gritted my teeth. Was I going to be able to say this out loud, this truth that was an untruth? How I thought Clare was conspiring when she was doing no such thing?

"Mum told me the next day that she and Dad had teamed me up with Clare to keep me here."

"Are you saying Clare was in on their plan?" His voice was hard.

Here goes. "I thought she was."

"You mean your anxiety thought she was."

"Yeah, that. I didn't ask her about it. I went away for the weekend. Everything ate at me. Every one of my fears and worries and doubts swallowed me whole and spat me out as an angry and paranoid freak."

"You should have called me."

I pushed away from the table. Maybe I should have pushed myself over the balcony and put us all out of our misery. "I'm a grown man. I shouldn't need to."

"Why not?"

"I should have my shit together by now."

"That's not how mental illness works. That's not how friendship works. Or did you forget we're friends?"

I sighed. Mike and I called each other often. We didn't need to wait for a *scheduled* call. We only scheduled calls so we couldn't say life got in the way. We talked outside of those calls whenever we liked. But my crazy brain hadn't thought of that.

"I can't even think like a normal person. These doubts keep on growing. They destroy my mind. And now I've destroyed everything."

"Define everything."

I stood up and paced, clutching at my hair.

"Beau, define everything."

I shook my head. Saying the words, facing the truth with Mike was too hard. Harder than facing it on my own? I stopped behind the chair and stared at the screen. "Clare."

"Tell me what happened with Clare."

I clutched at the top of the chair. "I called them all out on everything. I was so fucking angry. I accused Clare of conspiring with them."

I sank into the chair. Mike studied me. He must have thought I'd fucked up bad if he couldn't even speak to me.

"When did this happen?"

"A couple of days ago."

"And where's everything at now?"

"Clare's left me. I'm not speaking to my parents. I'm stuck in a job I don't want. Life sucks."

"You're still working at the orchard?"

"I can't leave now and prove them all right. Especially seeing as Clare has quit."

Mike shook his head. "You're staying there to spite them even though you're miserable?"

I shrugged. "I wanted to come back and work here. But not how Dad wants me to. Our visions don't align, and I don't know if they ever can."

"And that's your plan going forward? To stay?"

"What else am I supposed to do?"

"Be happy."

Happy—what a contrived piece of propaganda. I looked over at Dozer and smiled. At least something was good in the world.

"Beau."

I turned my attention back to Mike.

"Were you happy with Clare?"

"Yes."

"Explain that to me."

He reached out and touched the screen of his phone as if to dismiss a message.

"Explain to me how you were happy with Clare."

CHAPTER FORTY-TWO

Clare

I LAY on the couch with Clementine watching *Killing Eve.* The drama and death matched my mood. I hadn't been outside for days. The empty backyard reminded me that Beau and Dozer were gone. Everything reminded me that Beau and Dozer were gone. Clementine stretched and jumped down. I watched her walking up the hallway, glancing into rooms.

"They're not here."

She continued walking. Her ever-faithful puppy wasn't there to follow her. At least she'd stopped calling for him after the first couple of days.

I opened Beau's last message. *I'm leaving work now.*

His work, not mine. Everyone had gotten what they wanted. His mum and dad had him back. He was back in the business. Everyone had got what they wanted except me. I had no job. I'd wasted seven years of my life giving them everything I had. And I didn't have Beau. Who was I kidding? Beau and I were never going to last. It had been heading this way the whole time.

A car pulled up in the driveway. My heart jumped. I sat up and brushed the chip crumbs off my chest before answering the knock at the door. Tahlia stood there holding two six-packs of ciders.

"Hey, sis."

What was she doing here? I didn't want to talk to anyone. I went back into the lounge.

"Your decorating leaves a lot to be desired," she observed.

"Whatever." I didn't care about the mess—clothes strewn across the floor, dishes on the coffee table, empty glasses beside the couch.

"Have you just been wallowing for days?"

"Not much else to do."

Tahlia took the ciders to the fridge. She was wearing her PJs. I smiled. Tahlia was the type of person who'd pick up her pizza order in her pyjamas. She brought a couple of bottles over and handed one to me. Bloody Clint's brand. My stomach clenched. I opened the bottle and skulled half the contents.

"What are we watching?"

"*Killing Eve.*"

"Apt."

She took a few sips from her bottle. "Have you spoken to Beau?"

"No." Did we really need to speak about this? I downed the rest of my bottle.

"Why not?"

I rolled my eyes. "What's the point?"

"So you can talk about what happened."

What? Me telling him to fuck off? Or me saying he was

good at running away? Or rubbing it in that he was stuck with his parents, alone? Or me dumping his arse so quick he could have fractured his coccyx?

"He accused me of joining forces with his parents. He said I only pretended to like his ideas. I quit. I told him to leave. End of story."

"You're missing all the important parts." Tahlia finished her drink and went to get us another.

"They are the important parts. They're the only parts that matter."

Tahlia studied me as she drank her cider.

"Don't go making up shit," I said to her. "This was the way it was always going to end. Beau left."

"Although he didn't really leave, did he? You did."

"Semantics."

I turned my attention to the TV. I didn't want to talk about this or Beau.

I sighed. Even her silence pressured me to talk. "The fact is we were still living in our childhood memories. We can't live in the past."

I drank fast. Ugh. Why was Clint's cider so good? Arsehole.

"The past. Let's talk about the past. When you insisted Mum come home to die, Beau was there to support you the whole way. When you were busy with Mum, he was busy with me."

Beau always said I was his rock, but in actual fact, he was mine. He'd hugged me when I cried, stood and listened when I yelled in anger, made me laugh when I was sad.

I finished my second drink. My head was starting to feel fuzzy.

"The past is the past." I needed another drink.

"It isn't really the past. Beau was the same when he got home—kind, helpful, the same person we always knew."

I went to the fridge and grabbed another bottle. Tahlia was only halfway through her second one.

"Are you here to cheer me up or make me miserable?" I sank onto the couch.

"I'm here to tell you you're not alone."

I was alone. And I would remain that way. If it couldn't work with Beau, I didn't want it to work with anyone else.

"And I'm here to get drunk."

"Drink faster then."

THE BED WAS SWIMMING. Or the ceiling was swimming. Or I was swimming. I reached out, and my arm landed on the cold and empty space beside me. Beau was gone and wasn't coming back. I grabbed his pillow and hugged it to me. It still smelled like him.

I needed to wash the linen. He couldn't stay here with me forever. Not when he wasn't really with me. I held the pillow tighter and breathed in. How long would the smell last? If I kept breathing it in, would it wear away quicker?

The nights were the hardest. The silence was overwhelming. The thoughts running through my head wouldn't stay still. I went through all the signs I'd missed over the last eight months. His parents, their ideas for the future, how they included Beau and me in the same sentence. I'd trusted them. They were family. I didn't just lose Beau; I'd lost them too.

I threw the pillow away and grabbed my phone. I opened my email.

Dear Justin

No, not dear.

Justin,

I would like to fomraly tinder

Bloody hell. Alcohol and spelling didn't go together.

I would like to formally tender my resignation, effective immediately.

OK, that sounded professional enough. I supposed I should thank them even though I didn't want to.

Thank you for the opportunity of working at Hart Apples.

You stole my life and love away. You suck!

Clare

I hit send.

Hart Apples—good for your waist, even better for your heart. What a load of bullshit.

I rolled over and turned my back on the empty side of the bed.

CHAPTER FORTY-THREE

Beau

DOZER AND I WALKED DOWNSTAIRS. Andrew and Pete were sitting in the sun. When I'd first moved in, they hadn't asked me any questions. When I'd started managing them, they respected me enough not to ask where Clare was. Maybe they didn't think it was their place. They looked up as we approached.

"How are you today, Boss?"

"Good, thanks." I was far from good. "Do you have plans for today?"

"No, not really. We might play cards later."

"You can join us if you like," Pete said, giving me a lopsided grin.

"Yes, maybe. Thank you."

"Is Miss Clare coming back to work next week?" Andrew asked.

I wanted to say yes. But that would be a lie. "I'm not sure."

"OK."

"I'm going for a walk with Dozer. I'll see you when I get back."

"OK, Boss."

Dozer followed me into the orchard and then ran to the end of the row and back again. I admired his energy. I wish I had some. How had things gotten so bad? The real question was how had I fucked up so badly? The future I'd dreamed of with Clare was ruined. All because of my choices.

And those choices stemmed all the way back to when I'd decided to leave years ago. Part of me was trying to find myself and my place in the world. But the other part was me running away. I'd been running away from my parents, the orchard and Clare. I shook my head. Why would I run away from Clare, the person I wanted most in the world? Because I was scared she would reject me. Was that why I'd waited until the last day to kiss her?

That kiss. As perfect as it had been, it also ruined both of us in a way. A start that never had a chance to go further. It created a swarm of feelings that were left with nowhere to go. I'd created that.

Dozer barked. We'd reached the end of the row. He wanted to know which way to go. I pointed to the right. "That way."

He didn't bound off this time but stuck by my side. He kept looking up at me, concern in his golden-brown eyes. I gave him a half-hearted smile.

"I'm OK, boy." Another lie. Life choices made by my anxiety were the worst choices. Not answering Clare's call eight years ago—anxiety. Thinking I wasn't good enough—anxiety. Accusing Clare—anxiety. There was no way to come back from this. No way. Truth or anxiety? Truth.

Dozer and I kept walking. Maybe we would keep

walking forever, away from everything, away from here, away from Clare and our failed love. If I left, maybe Clare would come back to Hart Apples. She loved it here. She deserved to stay, to be happy.

Dozer yapped. I looked in the direction we were heading--Nan and Pop's house. My stomach clenched. They were two of the people I loved and respected most in the world, and they would be furious with me. And they had every right to be. I'd hurt their granddaughter again.

"Go on," I said to Dozer. He ran a million miles an hour in dog speed.

I took my time following him. When I reached the end of the trees, I stopped. Dozer was sitting next to Pop on the bench. They were both looking in my direction. My feet wouldn't move. A lump formed in my throat. I couldn't go to him. Pop should have the chance to chew me out. And I should have listened to him and taken it like a man. My feet wouldn't move. What a fucking weak excuse for a man.

I raised my hand and gave him a wave. He nodded in response. Then he told Dozer to come back to me. Dozer gave him a lick and came running. I turned and walked away.

CHAPTER FORTY-FOUR

Clare

I LAY IN BED, my eyes shut against the light. It was two in the afternoon, and I'd only left the bed to pee and feed Clementine. The rest of the world didn't exist for me anymore. What was Beau doing? I didn't deserve to know. I wasn't a good girlfriend or friend. I'd told him he could talk to me if he was anxious, but I shouldn't have left that up to him. I should have asked questions when I saw his mood change. I should have helped him speak up.

Beau deserved so much more than I'd given him. All his life, he'd deserved better. When we were kids, I should have helped him speak up. Instead of keeping it between us, I should have encouraged him. I was selfish then, and I was selfish now.

Not paying enough attention when he told me he didn't feel worthy was selfish. I should have spoken to him about it and told him he was deserving. I didn't, and that's exactly why I didn't deserve someone as good as Beau.

I sat up. I needed to go into town and buy some food,

especially cat food. I'd fed Clementine the last of it this morning. If I went now, in the middle of the day, I wouldn't run into Beau. He'd be at work.

That was a good plan. Go now.

I hopped out of bed and grabbed some clothes. Getting dressed in outside clothes was a novel idea. I'd worn pyjamas for the last week.

I dared to look in the bathroom mirror. My red hair was dull, my skin was pale and the bags under my eyes were hideous. A long, hot shower was in order, and makeup was a must. When I was ready to walk out the door, I was presentable, at least. Not like some apple left rotting under a tree.

As I drove into town, I scanned the cars that went past. Did I want to see Beau? A glimpse would both excite and terrify me.

I walked the aisles, aimlessly throwing things into the trolley. Whether there'd be the right ingredients to make a meal was a mystery. I pushed the trolley into the next aisle. Another trolley was coming out. We bumped.

"Sorry," I said as I manoeuvred the trolley to the left and kept going.

"Clare."

I knew that voice. Sharon. I pushed the trolley faster, yanking what I needed off the shelf and throwing it into the trolley.

"Clare," Sharon called after me.

I rounded the end of the aisle and into the next one. Sharon was at the other end waiting for me. For fuck's sake, I needed cat food, and it was where Sharon was standing. I powered down the aisle and stopped at what I needed.

Sharon approached. "How are you?"

Seriously? She wanted to make small talk? She'd ruined

my life and wanted to have a friendly little chat. I grabbed Clementine's food.

"I'd be better if you paid me my final pay."

"Clare—"

"I sent my formal resignation over a week ago. You've had ample time to pay me."

I gave her a cursory glance. She had tears in her eyes, eyes the same colour as Beau's. I groaned inwardly. Tears wouldn't get her anywhere. "Please make the payment by the end of the week."

I pushed off, paying her no further attention. Who the hell did she think she was? My former boss is who she was. Nothing more, nothing less. The fact that her smile had once warmed me and she'd made me feel special meant nothing anymore. Not since she'd also found a way to make me feel like shit. I clenched my jaw. As I rushed through the remainder of the store, I reminded myself to stop at the bottle shop. Running out of alcohol was not an option.

But no amount of alcohol would make me forget about Beau. Everything reminded me of him. The car and how he'd rest his hand on my leg. The shower and how showering together could be sweet or scorching hot. The stupid freaking lawn that he cared for better than I ever could. Alcohol numbed those memories, but it also brought tears.

I COULDN'T KEEP LIVING a life of luxury. Not that you could really call it a life of luxury—all I did was stay inside. I needed a job, not just for the money but for my sanity as well. But what job? I could stay in the apple industry and was sure I could find a job within a day if I put my mind to it. But did I want to work in apples if I wasn't at Hart Apples?

Many of my skills could be transferred to other agricultural industries. Or maybe I could go way left field and try something else. I started searching the job websites—administration, receptionist, customer service. Sitting in an office all day wouldn't suit my restless legs. Maybe I could work with animals. As long as none of the dogs reminded me of Dozer. I sighed loudly. It always led back to Beau.

How was he? And Dozer? I missed them both so much. The house didn't feel the same without them, like an apple orchard in winter. It was lifeless.

OK, working with animals was a bad idea for the moment. There was the Department of Agriculture. I had contacts there who I worked closely with through the nursery. Their fieldwork was interesting and something I had knowledge about. I would start there.

I stood up, moving Clementine off my lap. "Time to update my resume and make some calls."

Her eyes opened. She stared at me pointedly and then closed them again.

"Don't look at me like that. Beau could just as easily call me."

And I could very easily call him.

"He's the one who accused me of unimaginable acts."

Clementine yawned.

"I'm not being dramatic."

Nothing. No response.

"He should apologise for that."

I walked away. Clementine didn't even twitch.

CHAPTER FORTY-FIVE

Beau

ANXIETY LED to insecurities resulting in stupid fucking actions. Actions that, in my case, led to ruining more than one life. It was our life. I'd actually considered leaving when things had gone awry. The thing that Clare had feared the most. I'd fed her damn fear.

The phone rang. Mike's face appeared on my screen.

"How is everything, Beau?"

"No better," I admitted.

"It's been two weeks. If nothing's changed, I think we should put actionable plans in place."

I nodded. Those plans were a mystery to me. There was nothing that would get Clare back. Truth or anxiety speaking? I didn't know.

"Have you done any self-reflection?"

I assumed he knew the answer to that. My anxiety does nothing but self-reflect.

"Plenty. I know a lot of these problems stem from my

anxiety. It affects my self-esteem, my belief in myself and my relationships."

"Have you spoken to anyone about what's happened, apart from me?"

"No."

"Why not?"

"I'm finding it hard to face them."

Mike took notes. He was all business today.

"Do you think you should speak to your parents?"

Of course I should. But I didn't want to. It was too difficult. They'd knocked on the office door for the first few days, trying to get me to interact. Then they stopped. I pressed my hand against my leg. They'd tried to connect, and I'd shut down. "Yes, but I don't think it will work out well. I get too nervous and defensive."

Mike nodded. "I think we should schedule a call with them. If they want this to work out, they'll be willing. If not, well, we'll cross that bridge when we come to it."

Knowing Mike would be there was comforting. He had told me that when he first started speaking to his parents about his mental health, having Lisa there made it easier. "OK."

"What about Nan and Pop? Have you spoken to them?"

I shook my head.

"Why not? They've been very understanding and supportive."

"I don't want to see the disappointment on their faces."

It would be so much worse than my parents. Nan and Pop were my safe people. I had no right to ask them to forgive me for what I'd done to Clare.

"You're hiding from them."

I wasn't hiding, just avoiding. Who was I kidding? They were the same thing.

"It would be worse than facing my parents."

"You can't keep running, Beau. If they're important to you, then you need to prove it."

"I'll go and see them."

"I expect it to be done by the end of tomorrow. Text me to tell me how it went."

No one would ever say Mike wasn't persistent.

"OK."

"And what about Clare?"

I looked out the window at the newly greening orchard. Clare. I hadn't attempted to make contact. Sometimes I thought about it, but then I remembered her shock when I'd accused her of conspiring with my parents. And then her hurt. And then her undisguised anger.

"Beau?"

I brought my eyes back to Mike.

"What about Clare?"

"Neither of us has made contact."

"I think you should. You can't avoid her for another eight years. It's not fair on either of you."

"I know."

Clare deserved more from me. I needed to at least apologise to her. I needed to be the one to make contact with her. After all, I had started all this mess.

"OK. Your actions this week are to see Nan and Pop, have a meeting with your parents and make contact with Clare."

Sure wasn't much to ask.

"Before you go, I want you to watch this recording from our last session."

I tilted my head. I didn't remember him recording anything. I watched the screen. In the recording Mike said, "Explain to me how you were happy with Clare." I listened to my answer and watched my face as my frown turned into a smile.

TASK ONE: Visit Nan and Pop.

Pop was sitting under the tree when I pulled into the driveway. As soon as I opened the car door, Dozer jumped out and ran over to him. Pop gazed at me with his wise eyes. I gave him a wave before heading inside.

Nan was in the kitchen, stuffing a chicken. I watched from the doorway as she grabbed stuffing from a bowl.

"Hi, Nan."

Her head jerked up. She dropped the stuffing back into the bowl and came to me. I took a deep breath, not knowing what to expect. Nan took my face in her hands. The remnants of stuffing on her hands were cold and sticky. "Oh, my dear boy, we have missed you so much."

My heart swelled as tears leaked from my eyes. "I've missed you too, Nan."

She wrapped me in her arms. Her strength and comfort warmed me all the way to my toes. She stood back. When our eyes met, I saw her tears matched mine.

"Pop is under the tree. Go and get him and bring him inside."

I nodded. Pop. What the hell was I going to say to him? I walked outside and peered at him. He sat with Dozer, talking. Dozer glanced at him as he spoke and then looked out into the orchard. I pressed my hands against my legs, willing them not to shake.

"Hi, Pop," I said as I approached.

His head turned in slow motion. He gazed at me

without saying a word. My stomach dropped. He faced the orchard again.

"Come and sit, Beau." He tapped the bench beside him. My heart thundered in my chest. I sat stiff, my breaths shallow. Pop reached over and rested his hand on my shoulder.

"The voices, the anxiety in your head, what are they saying now?"

I rubbed my palms on my legs. "Nothing. They said enough on the way here."

Pop nodded. "You need to stop letting them take over."

"I thought I had."

"Clearly not."

"Clearly not."

Pop squeezed my shoulder. "What are you going to do about it?"

"About what?" Did he mean my anxiety? My life? Clare?

"The root of the problem."

My anxiety. "I need to speak up before the anxiety takes over. Is that what you did?"

"Yes. Thank God Nan was always there to listen."

Clare would have been there to listen if only I'd given her a chance. She'd told me so herself. She'd invited me to share my feelings with her. Instead, I'd shut her out. That wasn't fair. Instead of doubting her, I should have remembered those moments when she showed me she believed in me. Because then I would have realised that I was important. And I made a difference.

I make a difference. Me. My ideas are important.

Clare thought so too. Clare thought *I* was important.

"Have you spoken to Clare?" I asked.

"Clare has been as reclusive as you."

What? "It's been two weeks."

"We know. We miss her."

"I miss her too."

"Best you do something about it then."

"I have a plan."

"Let's hear it."

TASK TWO: Talk with my parents.

Mike contacted them and set up an online meeting. We would all be separate, which suited me. I'd moved from being sad to being angry. With them. And with myself. They owned their actions, but I owned my feelings. I'd forgotten that.

"Good morning," Mike said. "Justin, Sharon, thanks for joining us."

Dad stared stone-faced into the camera. Mum gave a small smile.

"Beau has explained to me that you all had a falling out recently. "

"You could call it that," Dad said.

"Would you like to explain that to me?"

"It was a misunderstanding."

I took a breath in. He'd want to say a bit more than just that.

Dad shifted in his seat. "I think there have been many misunderstandings throughout Beau's life."

"In what way?" Mike asked.

Mum put her hand on Dad's arm and said, "We've always wanted the best for Beau."

Here we go.

"That doesn't answer the question, Mum."

She turned to Dad. He patted her hand. He said, "It

was clear from a young age that Beau wasn't like other children. He was always thinking. Always watching."

"All kids are different," Mike said.

I let a harsh breath out. "What they're trying to say is that they didn't want me to be different."

"We didn't understand," Dad said.

"And you didn't listen. Like that stupid dinosaur party when I was seven. I told you I didn't want a party. I don't like parties. I don't like being the centre of attention. But you threw it anyway. Then you got angry with Clare and me when we hid away and had our own private party."

"It was rude. Your mother went to a lot of effort."

I sighed.

Mike glanced between us. "Do you think that situation could have been avoided if you'd listened to Beau?"

Dad's mouth was a thin line. His mouth twisted, and he nodded.

Miracles do happen.

"Are there other situations that could have been avoided by talking and listening?" Mike's voice was calm and hypnotic.

"I'm sure there are plenty."

"What about this latest one?"

Dad nodded.

"Why don't you tell me what happened?"

Mum sat up taller. "When Beau came back, we didn't want to lose him again, so we did everything we could to make him stay."

"And what were those things?"

"We teamed him up with Clare. We asked him to make a decision to move the business forward."

"Do you think that was a good idea?"

She paused. Her mouth moved, but nothing came out.

This was ridiculous. Why did Mike have to take it so slow with them?

I pressed my left hand against my leg. "Why would you want me to make a decision about the business? You never liked my ideas in the past."

"Is that true?" Mike asked.

"No," Dad said.

I rolled my eyes. "What are we even here for if we're not going to be honest?"

"We're here to make things better," Mum said.

"How can we make things better if we always avoid talking about what we think and what we feel?"

"There's no point overthinking everything," Dad said.

"I can't help overthinking everything," I said, my voice louder. "That's what anxiety does."

"What Beau is trying to say—"

"All I've ever needed is a bit of reassurance from you. When something was worrying me, you could have listened to me and spoken to me about it. Most parents would have, but all you did was ignore it."

"We didn't understand," Mum said.

"It was your job to understand," I said.

Mum looked down at the table.

"Clare understood. And she was a kid."

"That's why we teamed you up with her."

"No. You teamed me up with her because you're selfish. What you did to her was unfair. She gave you everything, and you would have cast her aside for me."

Mum and Dad looked at each other. Dad nodded. "You're right."

"There was more to the last disagreement," Mike said. "You didn't want him to leave again. I can understand that.

It must be hard having your child live so far away. What else happened?"

Dad shrugged. Mum twisted her hands. This was going nowhere.

"Beau?"

"All my life I've wanted my parents respect and acceptance. The fact they felt they needed to team me up with Clare showed me I didn't have that."

"What did it show you?"

"That they didn't think I could do this on my own."

Dad placed his palms down on the table. "That's not true."

What was true then?

"If I'd hired anyone else, I would have teamed them up with Clare. She knows the business inside out."

Oh.

"Beau," Mike said. I lifted my eyes back to the screen. He smiled at me. A safe, reassuring smile. "We're going to have to work more on this in coming sessions." He turned to my parents. "Beau has been so scared of your opinions and reactions in the past that when he feels you're putting him down, he doesn't speak up."

Dad shook his head. Not in an aggressive way. In a way to say he didn't understand.

"Beau has struggled with his mental illness. He has tried to open up with you, and he feels you have shut him down. We need to start talking openly about it and all of these other things."

Dad nodded. "Yes, we have a lot to talk about."

TASK THREE: Make contact with Clare.

Everything was ready. I knew what I wanted to say. All I needed to do was shove the fear of rejection aside. And I could do that for Clare.

I picked up my phone.

Hi Clare, can we catch up for a chat?

CHAPTER FORTY-SIX

Clare

I COULDN'T BELIEVE Sharon and Justin were sitting across from me on my front deck. We all stared at each other. They were the ones who wanted to talk. What were they waiting for?

"Clare, Sharon and I are sorry for making you feel unappreciated."

I continued to stare.

I wasn't sure what they were expecting me to say.

"We honestly didn't believe it would blow up like this," Sharon said.

I clenched my teeth. Did she think that made it alright?

Settle, petal, not everything was their fault.

"We didn't want to cause problems between you and Beau," Justin said. He ran his hand through his hair.

I looked between them. "There were a lot of problems between Beau and me. Unfortunately, many started with your actions."

Sharon glanced at her husband. He took her hand.

"We know, Clare. We put pressure on your relationship, and we put pressure on Beau. It was unfair."

"You weren't our only problem. We created our own too."

If they were here seeking my forgiveness, that was the best I could do. I wasn't ready to accept their apology in full. Not when they'd hurt Beau worse than they'd hurt me. I couldn't forget that yet.

Beau. The phone was burning a hole in my pocket. The message from Beau was burning a hole in my heart. I needed to speak to Nan and Pop.

I stood up. "Sorry, I need to go. Nan and Pop are expecting me."

Justin stood up. "Thank you for agreeing to see us."

I nodded. I was glad Sharon was on the other side of the table; otherwise, I might have hugged her. I didn't need her warmth confusing my brain.

"Have you offered Beau this same apology?"

"We have," Sharon said as she stood up. "We had a family session with his support person, Mike."

"His mental health support person," Justin clarified.

I nodded again. I wanted to know how that session went. They had a lot to work through as a family. A lot of resentment and hurt. Not to mention acknowledging Beau's mental illness. Counselling would do them good.

What would do me good was speaking to Nan and Pop.

I watched them leave and then went inside to grab my phone and keys. Clementine observed me from the couch. I picked her up and planted a kiss on her head. I swear she rolled her eyes at me. I smiled as I left the house.

I hadn't been lying when I said not all our problems stemmed from Sharon and Justin. Hell, my own thoughts had been sabotaging us from the start. I hadn't given Beau a chance. My thoughts were always about him leaving. They should have been about him staying. If he was having counselling sessions with his parents, did that mean he was staying? I shook my head as I pulled into Nan and Pop's driveway. That was the wrong question. He'd already told me he was staying.

I'd always thought that my job at Hart Apples made me who I was, and I'd be nothing if my job was taken away from me. But I was more than nothing. I was a million things beyond my job. When apple trees were pulled out of the ground, they weren't just dead apple trees. They were sustenance for future plantings. I didn't need Hart Apples to build a future for myself and Beau.

Nan and Pop were sitting in front of the TV, watching a game show. I sat on the couch. Pop turned the TV off.

"Nice of you to finally visit your old grandparents. We could be lying dead, and no one would have known."

"Lucky you didn't die then."

"Our favourite grandson came to visit us days ago."

My chest clenched. "How is he?"

"You could always ask him yourself," Nan said, her voice gentle.

I shook my head. "I'm not sure he'll want to speak to me."

"Why do you say that, love?"

"I haven't been very nice." That was an understatement. My parting shot about him running away and his parents had been cruel.

"Sometimes, when it gets heated, we say things we don't mean," Nan said.

My eyes widened. I couldn't imagine Nan and Pop ever being mean to each other.

"Don't look so surprised," Pop said. "We've been married a long time. It hasn't always been smooth sailing."

They were married, which meant they were obligated to work things out. Beau and I hadn't reached any significant milestones. We didn't have to make anything work. Except I wanted to. Did Beau? It wasn't only the cruel words we needed to get past.

"What did Beau say?"

Nan came and sat beside me. That wasn't good. "Beau—"

"You should ask him yourself," Pop said.

After Nan's reaction, I wasn't sure I wanted to. But we couldn't start to make it right if I didn't risk anything.

"What will I say to him? I screwed up pretty bad."

There weren't just the words I'd said. There were the words I didn't say. Like how I didn't defend myself harder against his accusations. It was like he'd given me an out, and I took it. I left before he could.

"I'm sure you'll figure it out," Pop said.

"Start with how you're feeling. Talk openly about what happened. Be honest but kind. Say sorry."

"I can do that." I could do anything for Beau.

Pop stood up. Was he trying to get rid of me?

"Off you go. He's waiting under the tree."

"What?" My stomach lurched.

"He's waiting for you under the tree."

Shit. I wasn't ready for this. My hand went to my hair.

"He's not here to see your hair."

"OK." I shook my hands out. I needed to breathe. "OK." I walked to the door. My stomach was still in my throat. I swallowed the lump.

Beau stood up as soon as I stepped out into the backyard. He watched me the whole way across the lawn. Talk about being in the spotlight. How did runway models handle this? My stomach churned.

"Hi." He gave me a small smile.

My heart lifted. I wanted to embrace him and feel him against me. I would probably never let go. Almost three weeks without the man who held my heart had been hard. But holding him right now was jumping way too far ahead.

Beau reached out and touched my hair. "Nice colour."

Royal blue. "It reminds me of someone I love."

"He loves you just as much."

It was so easy for him to declare his love for me. But how could he say that when I hadn't apologised yet?

Beau took my hands. "I'm sorry I was such an arse. I should have spoken to you when my brain started to go into overdrive."

"I should have spoken to you too instead of pushing you away." I couldn't leave it at that. I turned to the bench. "Let's sit down." We sat next to each other, close, touching. "When you came back, there were two things I was worried about—you taking my job and you leaving again."

"I never wanted to take your job. I only wanted to work with you."

And look where we were now. Rash Clare had made her mark again.

Beau kicked at the ground with his toe. "If you want to come back to Hart Apples but don't want to work with me, I will leave. I'll work with Clint if that makes you happy."

"I don't think it'll come to that." I held Beau's hand tighter. "I'd fallen for you so hard; I was scared to lose you again."

The bees buzzed in our silence. What was Beau thinking?

"I'm not going anywhere, Clare. I want to stay here with you."

"But not at Hart Apples?"

"Not if it's going to cause friction between us."

"What about your parents? Do you think it will work with them being so invested in the business?"

Beau sighed. "I don't know. I would have been happy to come back and work at the orchard, but I'm not sure I can give them what they want."

"Do you want to give them more?"

Beau shrugged. I shook my head. I knew exactly what he was thinking.

"You need to start putting yourself and your mental health first. If they can't respect that, don't make it your problem."

"Thank you."

"I don't know if I want to return. You're more important to me than Hart Apples." I moved closer to him. "I'm sorry I didn't trust you."

"Trust goes both ways. I wasn't very good at it either."

"I was terrified you were going to leave. I should have spoken to you about it earlier, before your dad brought it up." I looked at Beau. He was already watching me. "It came out in the worst way possible."

He nodded. My chest tightened.

"I'm sorry, Beau. I know it must have felt like you were being ganged up on. I was too selfish to realise it."

"It's OK." Beau rubbed his thumb over my knuckles. "My anxiety didn't help. I should have said something when it started nagging at me."

"We can do better," I said.

"I want to do better." Beau smiled at me. "And I can. If

I've learnt anything through all of this, it's that my doubt in myself made me doubt you."

The sun was starting its descent over the orchard.

"I'm sorry, Clare. I should never have accused you of conspiring with my parents. You had every right to be angry."

"Telling you to fuck off wasn't my greatest moment."

"I deserved it. I know you are the last person on Earth who would ever do something like that to me."

Beau pulled me up. We stood close. I missed this, being in his space. He stepped closer and tilted his head to mine. His earthy smell made me giddy. His lips met mine, soft and lingering. Lightness spread throughout my body.

Beau pulled away, and I reached out to pull him back. He smiled but shook his head. "I want to show you something first." He took my hand and led me to the treehouse ladder. He wanted to show me the treehouse? "Go on."

I climbed the ladder with Beau directly behind me. My head emerged through the hole in the floor. My feet stopped moving. The interior was lit with fairy lights. Cushions and blankets covered the floor. And the walls were adorned with photos of Beau and me throughout the years as children and teenagers, as well as pictures from the last few months.

Tears sprung to my eyes.

CHAPTER FORTY-SEVEN

Beau

I GAVE Clare's butt a small shove to encourage her to keep moving. She made it onto the floor and began wandering from wall to wall, looking at the photos. I made my way to the cushions in the corner and watched her. My heart filled as she fingered the photos and smiled to herself. Every now and then, she'd glance at me with a wondrous smile on her face.

"Did you do all of this?" she asked.

"Yes."

"It's beautiful."

I'd got the photos all together the day before and was preparing myself to ask Clare to meet me when Pop had texted to say she was already here. I was so bloody nervous I'd half walked, half ran here.

She left the last of the photos, came to me, and straddled my lap. She continued smiling and looking around. "I love you, Beau. This is amazing. You're amazing."

"I'm not afraid anymore, Clare. I'm not afraid to give you my heart. I know I can trust you with it."

Clare rested her hands on my shoulders and leant in. Her body pressed against mine as our lips met. There was something else I needed to do, but all thoughts were blocked out by her lips. And the warmth of her as she pressed against my groin shattered any remaining resolve. My hands went to—

"Are you two still alive?" Pop called out. He sounded far away, probably at the kitchen door.

Clare sat up. "Yes."

"Glad you haven't killed each other. Have you done it yet?"

That was a question for me.

"No," I answered.

Clare tilted her head. "Done what?"

"Dinner will be ready in twenty."

"OK," I called out.

The back door closed.

"Done what?" Clare asked.

This was it. I took a deep breath. I should have been terrified, but I wasn't. "All these photos, they're a part of our past."

She glanced around.

"I want to make more memories with you. Forever. Will you marry me?"

I shimmied her back a little, so I could get the ring out of my pocket and held it out to her. Clare took it from me and held it like it was something fragile.

"That's Nan's ring."

"Nan and Pop want us to have it."

Tears welled in her eyes.

I couldn't have asked for a more perfect token of love.

Nan and Pop had been married for a long time, and they loved each other now as much as they had that first day. I wanted to build a future like that with Clare.

Clare still held the ring. She was silent.

"Well?"

She grinned as her attention turned from the ring to me. "Oh, you want an answer?"

"It would be nice."

She slipped the ring on her finger. "Yes, Beau, I want forever with you."

She pushed me against the wall. Her body followed, and this time her lips weren't just eager but hungry too. She pulled her lips away just a little. Her breath tickled mine. "Shall we consummate our engagement?"

"Isn't that a marriage thing?"

"It's a whatever-we-want-to-make-it thing."

"You took so long to decide, we only have fifteen minutes."

"Plenty of time."

EPILOGUE

Beau

I SAT under the apple tree, waiting for Clare. This was our half of the orchard. Mum and Dad had agreed to subdivide it. We retained Nan and Pop's original orchard, including the nursery. It was a good deal, allowing us to share resources with my parents while running our own separate business. It was helpful to my relationship with them too, being close but not too close. And being able to do our own thing.

Nan was watering her flower garden. She wore loose green pants and a bright pink top. If she were any smaller, we'd lose sight of her. She blended in so well with her colourful blooms. Pop was in the vegetable garden planting seedlings. The scarecrow we'd restuffed after Dozer had attacked it stood tall above him.

It was nearing the end of winter, and the bees would re-emerge soon. The orchards would come alive again with bees and flowers and workers. I looked out into our orchard and smiled. Life was good.

Clare pulled up beside the house and got out of the car. Nan and Pop looked in her direction and then continued their work. They must have been enthralled by what they were doing to not even call out a hello, which was weird.

Clare went around to the back of the ute and called out, "Turn around. I have a surprise for you."

I turned and faced the orchard. As I did, I noticed that Nan and Pop had stopped what they were doing and were walking towards each other. Clare approached, her footsteps slow. I wanted to turn to see what she was doing, but I wasn't going to risk getting the Clare Stare. Her footsteps stopped a few feet away from me.

"OK, turn around."

I turned slowly. Clare stood there smiling, an apple tree at her feet. "I present to you our first Fanny."

A Geeveston Fanny. We'd chosen this heirloom variety mainly because of its charming name. And it was a Tasmanian apple. And it was great for pies.

I took a few steps towards the tree. This was it, our first change in the guard. Two years of hard work and she was ready to plant. All because Clare believed in my vision as much as I did. She managed to make me the happiest man in the world every day, and this topped it off.

"Mrs Hart, I think you've outdone yourself." I gave her a hug.

A flash of white caught my eyes. There was something attached to the trunk. I couldn't make it out. I bent closer. It was plastic and rectangular. I untied it and examined it. The word *pregnant* and two little lines jumped out at me.

My heart was in my throat. I tried to swallow it back down. Clare's grin was contagious, and so were her tears. And we weren't the only ones crying. Nan and Pop, who'd arrived a moment before, hugged each other with tears rolling down their cheeks.

I embraced Clare, holding her tight. This woman made every single one of my dreams come true.

"Must be the magic of the treehouse," Pop said.

Our heads whipped around.

"Shoosh, don't tease the children," Nan said, giving him a nudge.

"It's not my fault their secret rendezvous up there aren't so secret."

What the hell? I was sure they'd been out the last time we'd come for a little fun. Pop gave us a crooked grin. Bloody old man was pulling our leg.

"You're just jealous that you can't get up there anymore," Clare said.

"Don't need a treehouse. We have a perfectly good bed."

I met Clare's gaze and smiled. My ambition in life was for us to be like Nan and Pop in our seventies. I had no doubt Clare could make that dream come true too.

OTHER books available in the Love Down Under Series are:

The Cat's Out of the Bag

She's started a new life. He's escaping his. Can two tortured souls find a future together?

Evie's a survivor. After rebuilding herself and her life, she's feeling the one thing she never thought she would – happy.

Until Jesse...

When she meets Jesse while volunteering at a cat shelter, dark memories of her past return. She is stronger now and wants to trust him, but after all she's been through, is trust even possible?

Jesse's a self-made billionaire yearning to get away from his empty life and the money-hungry parasites who inhabit it.

The plan?

Go to sunny Australia, leaving his old life behind, to find himself. But instead of finding just himself, he finds Evie, who is everything anyone should aspire to be. Now, what he aspires to be, is hers.

But to be hers, he needs to tell her everything and putting his heart on the line is hard.

The quest to find a cat a forever home leads them to travel across the country together. Will they find the strength to confide in each other? Or will the close quarters drive them apart?

Let Sleeping Dogs Lie

When she left him...

...Tara couldn't explain why.

After five years, did she still have feelings for Shepherd?

Her brother's passing hit Tara hard and it left a scar. That night, at the party, when she saw Shepherd high, Tara had no choice, it was over. It brought up too many painful memories and she wouldn't go through it again. The decision was simple.

She had to leave.

No goodbye.

For Shepherd, losing Tara broke his heart. Not knowing why she left, well that pain he addressed with drugs, alcohol, and meaningless relationships. After he hit rock bottom, he cleaned up and came up with a plan to get her back. Could it work?

It was his only shot.

Would a desperate ruse, with the best intentions, but costing a fortune, give him the chance to win her heart for good? Or would it ruin him?

Will she be brave enough to be loved?

Get Off Your High Horse

When two opposites collide will their differences ignite a spark?

Frankie and Sebastian live totally different lives. Lives that are entwined through polo, the sport of kings. How entangled will they become?

Australian farmgirl, Frankie, has no interest in high society or the rich, arrogant riders she has to deal with, especially Sebastian. Her heart may be softening to his kindness and love of horses, but her brain won't be convinced. She's looking forward to her summer break on the farm, away from him...

...until her parents invite Sebastian to stay.

Sebastian never felt comfortable in his role as the Crown Prince of Oleander. He'd rather spend his days working with horses, playing polo and being with Frankie, whose fiery spirit has set his heart aflame.

But pressure from his mother, the Queen, to return to his royal duties is mounting. Everything he desires is in danger of being ripped away.

Can Sebastian convince Frankie that his hopes and dreams aren't so different from hers, or is he destined to return to a life he doesn't want, alone?

Love and secrets are a tricky combination

For Emily, going home isn't easy, especially when her small town never felt like home in the first place. She escaped Alma seven years ago when she went to university, but now her estranged father needs her help. At least returning means spending time with the only good thing in town—her best friend, Luke.

Luke always knew Emily needed to be free of their hometown, so he withheld his true feelings. Even though she has returned, he knows she will never stay. He tries hard to respect the boundaries of their friendship but every moment they spend together makes it harder to deny their connection. Self-control dissipates. One kiss turns into two...

But is Luke really the man Emily remembers? When Emily discovers Luke has betrayed her trust, they could lose the most precious thing of all—each other.

A Bird In The Hand

She yearns for the past. He wants a better future. Can they learn to love the present together?

When thirty-something Makayla's long term boyfriend pulls the 'let's have a break' card she is left broken hearted. Her best friends seize the opportunity and book a bus tour up the west coast of Australia. They hope distance will give her perspective, but she can't see past what she's lost.

Tyson needs a break from work and relationships, if that's what you can call them. When his mates plan the trip of a lifetime he decides to tag along. He's sure it will get him out of his rut, and and in turn, help him set a course for his future.

No one is prepared for the planning mishap that finds Makayla and Tyson sharing a room together. Their personalities clash – she's always too serious and he just wants some lighthearted fun. Add a fouled mouthed cockatoo to the equation and the perfect trip is not so perfect. Or is it?

ACKNOWLEDGMENTS

Cover by 100 Covers
Edited by Tegan Holmberg
Proofread by Half Caff Press
And thanks to my amazing beta readers

ABOUT THE AUTHOR

Cynthia is a document controls manager by day and a writer by night. She enjoys writing about places she visited with her daughter while they travelled around Australia. She says that travel and reading are the best educators. Still, to this day, they both enjoy travelling and reading. A love of animals sees them feature in her books, some have small parts, others larger.

Find her online: http://cynthiaterelst.com/

All of her social links can be found here, Linktree: https://linktr.ee/cynthiaterelst

www.ingramcontent.com/pod-product-compliance
Lightning Source LLC
Chambersburg PA
CBHW020910130726
47904CB00006BA/1809

9780648729457